HARD TO TACKLE

HARD
TO
TACKLE

by GILBERT DOUGLAS

jD7456h

Thomas Y. Crowell Company
New York

For my nephew,
Gilbert Daladin Douglas

HARD TO TACKLE

CHAPTER ONE

CLINT THOMAS awoke to the sound of his father's call from downstairs. It was late afternoon and his bedroom was hot. He lay there on his bed for a few moments, sweating and groggy.

"Clint!" his father's voice came again. "Let's hear some signs of life up there."

Clint jumped from his bed and hurried through dressing and combing his hair. He went down to dinner with his eyes full of sleep, feeling grouchy. He wasn't used to napping in the afternoon. Today had been an exception because he had worked in a hayfield in the country until three o'clock. And since he was swimming tonight, he figured he could use a couple of hours of sleep.

Because it was hot, Clint's mother served dinner on the screened back porch, bringing the food from the kitchen.

"Got through work early today," his father said.

"Yeah. I'm through for the season, Dad. I've turned in my pitchfork. We finished at Old Man Finch's place and he paid me off." He smiled. "I'm glad it's over."

"Well, you're hardened up for football. That's what you wanted."

"That's right," Clint agreed. "But it's been a long summer."

They ate in silence for a couple of minutes, and then his father said, "Are you going to make a showing to-night?"

An uncomfortable feeling came over Clint. But he shrugged his shoulders carelessly. "Probably not," he admitted.

"You don't seem much concerned," his father said. "I saw your coach yesterday. He told me that you've missed practice a number of times."

Clint looked at his father. George Thomas did not look his age. His hair was thick, crisp and sandy. Despite the fact that, as a drugstore proprietor, he did not get much exercise, his body was slender. He had a square-jawed face, a face that suited his personality. Clint remembered the picture of his father in the foot-ball section of an old State College yearbook. He stood on spread feet, hands on hips, his strong jaw thrust out as though he challenged all comers. He had been very slender and he must have been good to hold down a regular berth on the varsity.

"I've been working steady," Clint said. "Sometimes I was too tired to go to practice in the evenings."

[2]

"But not too tired to go chasing around with Ralph Vanderpool."

Clint didn't say anything. His excuse had sounded thin, and it was thin. He had skipped practice with no real justification except that there had been things he wanted to do more.

His mother was speaking now, sticking up for him. "I think Clint has done very well. I'm surprised that he's had time for swimming at all. Some boys Clint's age don't do anything but enjoy themselves. Like Ralph. He hasn't done anything all summer but play tennis and ride around in that new car of his."

"Ralph is lazy," George Thomas said bluntly.

Anger rose in Clint. After all, Ralph was his best friend, and his father knew it. There was an edge to his voice. "Why should Ralph go out and sweat in the hayfields like I have? He doesn't need the money. His dad gives him all he needs. Anything he wants, he gets. There are plenty of fellows in this town who wouldn't work in the fields on a bet. That's why the government lets Mexican nationals come in every summer."

George Thomas laid down his fork and looked squarely at Clint. "Now wait a minute—"

Clint knew that tone of voice. It always preceded an argument, or ended it. Clint drew in his neck.

"Nobody forced you to go out and work on the farms," his father said. "It was your choice. Maybe it was just an excuse so that you could buy a car. You got your own way, and you found the work a little harder than you expected. So now, you want to feel sorry for yourself."

Clint opened his mouth to say something back, but his mother interrupted. "Now, now, let's not have any arguments at the dinner table. I forbid it. You're both cranky. It's the heat."

His father didn't say any more. After a couple of minutes of uncomfortable silence, Clint tried to clear the air by talking about a boy he had been working with in the fields.

"His name's Paul Slansky," Clint said. "His folks are some kind of foreigners. His mother's nice but I can hardly understand the old man's lingo. They moved up here from California last spring and he's in my class. He says he played football down there, and he looks like good material. He's heavy-built, but he can move fast. I've been trying to get him to say that he'll turn out for football, but he's got the idea that he wants to work on Saturdays this fall. Then, he lives out there by the river, and if he turns out for practice he misses the school bus and hasn't got any way to get home."

"Perhaps something can be worked out," his father said soberly.

Clint eyed the big apple pie on the table. It was brown on top and there were little sugary bubbles coming through. It made his mouth water. Reluctantly he decided that he wouldn't eat any, because he was swimming. He excused himself and left the table. He was feeling alive now and he didn't want to leave with any unpleasantness between him and his father.

[4]

"Coming to the pool tonight, Dad?" he asked.

His father looked up and smiled and winked at him. "Sure, Son, we'll be there."

Clint left the house and headed up the sidewalk toward Ralph's home, three blocks away. He was thoughtful as he walked along. He wished he was ready for the races tonight. It would please his father if he should win.

One reason he had missed practice so many times was that he wanted to keep Ralph for a friend. Clint knew that most grownups thought Ralph was spoiled and conceited. But Ralph wasn't so bad. What they thought was conceit was simply self-confidence. He wasn't spoiled either. It was just that Ralph's father gave him more freedom than most fellows had.

The Vanderpool home was large and modern. Ralph's cherry-red convertible was parked at the curb in front. The Vanderpools were prominent, well-to-do people in the city of Monroe. Mr. Vanderpool was a contractor who built homes. He was a capable business man, and he made money.

Clint found Ralph in the back yard, stretched out in a hammock, listening to dance music on a portable radio.

"Hi, old buddy," Ralph drawled. "How's the farmer? Comb the hayseed outa your hair and visit with a city dude."

Clint grinned, feeling good. He took a lawn chair and stretched his long legs out before him.

The boy in the hammock was rangy and dark. Clint

had once heard someone call him "hawk-featured." The name fitted. His nose was high-bridged and sharp, a little too large. His black eyes were deep set. But they could shine with humor, as they did now.

"We'll be playing football in a coupla weeks," Clint said. "You'd better put that hammock away and start doin' some road work."

Ralph waved his hand and grimaced, as though such a thing was not to be thought of. Clint laughed aloud. It was this easy-going trait in Ralph that he admired. And Ralph got away with it. Last year he had been the hottest player on the Monroe team. He was a halfback, a flashy runner.

They talked and listened to the music for nearly an hour. They could laugh over nothing, just because they were young and cocky.

"What time do you have to be at the pool?" Ralph asked then.

Clint glanced at his watch. "Swimming won't start until eight. But we might as well get going."

They strolled around to the front of the house and climbed into the shiny new convertible. Ralph started the car and pulled away from the curb. The twin mufflers made a throaty purr.

"Are you going to win tonight?" Ralph asked.

Clint shrugged. "The team might. I doubt if I will."

"I don't see why you mess around with this swimmin', buddy. You're no great shakes as an athlete. Why waste your time?"

Clint frowned and bit his lip. For years Ralph had been telling him that he wasn't much of an athlete. Maybe he was right, but did he always have to keep rubbing it in?

"If you're so hot, why didn't you turn out for the team?" Clint grumbled.

Ralph laughed and gave him a playful poke in the ribs.

Shortly after eight o'clock, Clint stood on the runway at the edge of the municipal pool. He had on red swim trunks. His torso was tanned and muscular. He was near six feet, and well developed for his seventeen years.

Music, which sounded thin and tinny, was coming over the public address system. The white corks that supported the lane markers bobbed on the jade-green water of the pool. The lanes ran across the pool's width. There was a good-sized crowd in the bleachers across the pool.

Suddenly the music stopped, and the announcer's voice came over the speaker. "First call for the girls' one-hundred-yard freestyle. Swimmers report to the starter's gun."

Clint watched five girls, two in red suits and three in black, move to the edge of the pool. He spoke to a tall, tanned girl in a red suit. "Good luck, Judy."

She smiled at him, showing teeth that were white and even. Her name was Judy Harlin, and she was the best girl swimmer on the Monroe team.

"Swimmers take your marks!" called the starter. "Get set!" . . . *Bang!* With the gun, five lithe bodies hit the water and the race was on.

Clint watched Judy boil along, arms lifting and falling and legs thrashing with perfect rhythm. At the end of the first lap she was ahead by a yard. She made her turn with the quick, smooth grace of a seal. At the end of the third lap, it was no longer a race as far as Judy was concerned. She was too far ahead. But everyone's eyes were on the girl. The way she was surging along, she might set a new record—if she could keep up the pace.

Watching her, Clint thought she wasn't hurrying at all. Her form was perfect, and her amazing speed was deceptive. Like all fine athletes, she made it look easy. Only by comparing her position with that of the other swimmers could he realize how fast she was going. He was tense as she turned into the last lap. Could she keep up that blistering pace?

"Pour it on, Judy!" he yelled hoarsely. "Keep going, kid."

She came down the homestretch in a spray of arms and legs. She never slackened her pace. The crowd was on its feet cheering her. They knew that they were watching more than just an ordinary girl swimmer. When she slapped the concrete at the finish, the crowd let out a happy sigh and sat down. Clint reached down, took her hand and lifted her from the water in one long motion. Her face beamed with elation as she turned up the sides of her white swim cap and brushed the water from her eyes.

Clint looked at her with strong admiration. "Golly, you really moved. The time was fast."

When the others had finished, there was a hush of expectancy as everyone waited to hear the time.

The voice finally came from the speaker. "Ladies and gentlemen, the results of the girls' one-hundred yard freestyle: Harlin, Monroe, first; Lynch, Stanwood, second; Walters, Monroe, third; and Smith, Stanwood, fourth." There was a pause, and the voice went on. "The winning time was one minute and ten seconds. Ladies and gentlemen, the winning time for this event sets a new state record. But we understand that this time will not be officially recognized as a new record because this is not a state meet. Miss Harlin will get her chance next Friday at the state meet in Urbana."

There were cheers and applause from the bleachers.

"Nice going, Judy," Clint said.

"Let's see you win," she challenged.

"I'll try," he said, but his voice sounded hollow and unconvincing.

He desperately wished that he was prepared for this race. Right now, he wanted to win the 100-yard free-style more than anything. But it would be a miracle if he did.

When he took his place at the pool's edge, a small hope rose in him. Maybe he could win. He was in superb physical condition. He'd have to remember not to take the early laps too fast, and then run out of gas. Timing was very important. But timing, he knew, came from long and careful practice.

The starter's voice cut through his thoughts. "Swimmers, take your marks! . . . Get set! . . ." Eager bodies crouched, faces uplifted. With the crack of the gun, Clint launched himself forward in a shallow racing dive. Gliding out of the dive, he went into his crawl stroke. Five laps to go!

He was in the third lane and a glance at the end of the first lap told him that they were all nearly even. As he made his turn at the end of the second lap, the hope in him rose a little further. Only one man was ahead of him. He breathed, stroked, felt the water gliding past his body. The shouts of the crowd reached him as a dull roar. He made his turn. He felt the first traces of heaviness come into his arms. He seemed strangely alone. A swimmer had nothing to rely upon except his training and his will. You could lean on your teammates when the going got rough in some sports—but not in swimming. You were completely on your own.

The others were inching ahead of him. He tried to keep up, but it was no go. Inexorably, they left him behind. The smooth beat of his stroke wavered with the beginning of fatigue. When he flipped over at the turn for the last lap, he had dropped back into fourth place. He put all his remaining energy into an attempt to catch up. But he had lost his form and he was wasting effort. His arms would not do what he wanted them to.

[10]

His legs were weighted. He came in a sorry fourth. He grabbed the edge of the pool with both hands and hung there in the water, lungs laboring for air.

When he lifted himself out of the water, his eyes met Judy's. She smiled at him. "Don't look so sad, Clint. You tried."

He made a grimace of disgust. Coming in last was a blow to his pride and self-confidence. He stood with hands on hips, while his shoulders rose and fell with the force of his breathing. He saw Ralph sitting beside a girl over in the bleachers. Ralph was smiling at him —or was he laughing? Clint suddenly felt angry. It was Ralph who had influenced him to miss practice. It was Ralph who had said, "Come on, let's catch that movie. It won't hurt you to miss one night's practice. Come on, a little recreation will do you good."

And because he was in the habit of letting Ralph make decisions for him, Clint had listened and followed. There was always tomorrow night to practice. He did not stop to think that the season would not last forever.

But as the announcer called the swimmers for the next race, he knew that he was passing the buck. He was old enough to make up his own mind. There was no sense in blaming Ralph.

He did a little better in the 60-yard backstroke. He came in third among six swimmers. Walt Tracy, a friend of Clint's, took first for Monroe in the 440-yard freestyle. Judy won the girls' event at the same distance, and again shaved time off the state record. She got a big hand when the announcement was made.

As the events moved by, it seemed to Clint that the red and black teams were pretty evenly matched. When the men's 160-yard freestyle relay, the last event, was over, they crowded around the judges. Clint didn't hear the score announced, but he read the verdict in Walt Tracy's eyes as Walt turned around.

"They beat us by nine points," Walt said.

Clint wasn't pleased as he headed for the dressing room. He hadn't been much help.

Swimmers were still standing around in groups, talking things over, when he came out of the dressing room. The Monroe crowd seemed rather happy for a losing team. But that was because of the showing Judy Harlin had made. She was excited, and her eyes sparkled. It was funny about her eyes. Clint guessed that they were blue, but sometimes they had a greenish tint so that he wasn't quite sure what color they were. Her brown hair was wet and lay close to her head in dark waves.

He wished that he had his own car so that he could take her home. There was Ralph's car but, for some reason, Judy and Ralph were not friendly.

The bleachers on the far side of the pool were empty. Clint saw Ralph standing near the entrance gate, waiting. As Clint started off, Walt grabbed his arm.

"Anybody with you and Ralph?" he asked.

"Nope."

Walt grinned. "Then how about riding downtown with you, old pal? You wouldn't want a fellow swimmer to walk all the way to town, would you? I'm beat."

"Sure, Walt. Come along."

They rode downtown in the open car with the soft night air moving around them. The lights along the street shone bright and cheerful.

"Well, we may not take the state meet," Walt was saying, "but I'll bet we have the best girl swimmer at the meet. Judy is going places—and she deserves it. She's worked hard to get as good as she is. Man, she glides through the water like a trout!" He wagged his head. "It's funny about that girl. She don't look much like an athlete. She's almost delicate. But she's got that old drive. She's a good competitor."

Clint's voice was suddenly rough. "I don't think I'll go to the State. I sure wasn't any help to the team tonight."

"Aw, Clint," Walt said. "You've got a whole week to get in some extra practice. Besides, we haven't got anyone to take your place."

Clint made no answer.

"Get your chin off the floor, Clint," Ralph said laughingly. "So you didn't come in first. So what? It's not important. Tomorrow there'll be a small write-up in the paper and your name will appear in fine print along with the others. In a week no one will be able to tell you who won and who lost."

Walt scowled. "Sure, it's important. What's getting your name in the newspapers got to do with it? We swim because it's fun."

"Rah—rah—rah," Ralph said sarcastically.

Walt looked at him with irritation. "If it's all a lot of foolishness, how come you play football?"

"Well, football is different. You get headlines in football, and a lot of other advantages. Makes you a big man around school—you know? Makes the girls think you're just adorable. Football pays off. These minor sports don't. You're not going to see me busting my lungs just for what you call fun."

Walt clammed up, but Clint had to laugh. Ralph was smooth and clever, and there weren't many who could win an argument with him. And maybe he was right, Clint thought. Maybe it wasn't very important.

"I think you're just jealous because you aren't on the swimming team," Walt muttered finally.

"Pooh," Ralph said.

He swung the car into the drive-in. It was crowded and they had to pull far over on one side. Ralph switched off the ignition and flicked the lights for service. From where they were parked, Clint could see into a back room of the building. A colored boy sat on an upended box peeling potatoes into a big pot.

"Isn't that Jeff Washington?" Clint said.

Walt looked ahead. "Yeah. That's Jeff."

"I didn't know he worked here."

"Neither did I," said Walt.

Jeff Washington's shoulders looked huge as he bent over the pot. Clint said, "I wonder why he has never turned out for sports at school."

Walt shrugged. "I doubt if anyone except Coach Sullivan ever gave him any encouragement. Sully told me that he asked Jeff to come out for football, but Jeff refused. Wouldn't give a reason. Maybe he's afraid there would be trouble."

"Naw, there wouldn't be any trouble. There are Negroes on athletic teams everywhere. It must be some other reason."

"There's never been a Negro on a Monroe team. That might make a difference."

"I don't think so," Clint said.

Walt kept looking at Jeff. "His dad was a big athlete at Southern Cal. Football and track. Jeff handles himself like an athlete. I'll bet he'd be great if he wanted to."

Ralph turned on the car radio. The carhop walked up with her order pad. She was a junior at Monroe. She looked with admiration at the new car and smiled at Ralph who kidded with her as they gave their orders.

They listened to music while they waited for their food. Jeff Washington left his seat and came out to a shed and grabbed a sack of potatoes. Walt stuck his head around the edge of the windshield. "Hey, Jeff," he called.

The boy looked around curiously. He let go of the sack and walked over to Walt's side of the car. He was a tall boy with big hands and long arms. He showed his teeth in a handsome smile. "Hi, Walt." He nodded at Clint and Ralph.

"Hi, Jeff," Clint said. "How's it with you?"

Jeff waited a moment before answering. Ralph had not spoken. A faint hostility came into Jeff's dark eyes as he looked at Ralph. But his voice was pleasant as he spoke. "Okay, Clint. How's it with you?"

"Pretty good."

Jeff took a clean handkerchief from his trousers and wiped his perspiring face. "Cooling off out here," he said, "but still hot back there." And he jerked his head toward the room where he had been working.

"Coming out for football this year, Jeff?" Walt asked.

Jeff looked away. "I—I reckon not."

"You're missing a lot of fun, boy. With those hands of yours, I bet you could snatch a pass out of the air one-handed."

Jeff looked thoughtfully down at his hands. "These hands better get back to peeling spuds. See you fellas."

He turned and went back to the sack of potatoes. He lifted it easily and carried it into the back room.

Their hamburgers and milk shakes arrived. Walt took a big swallow from his glass and said, "Coach Sullivan is back in town. He spent all summer driving a bull-dozer on a construction job upstate. You won't know him. Brown as an Indian, and tough-looking. I saw him yesterday."

"What'd the old coot have to say?" Ralph asked.

"He asked me what I'd been doing all summer. When I told him I'd been working in a grocery store and swimming, he didn't look happy at all. He said, 'You boys better be getting in some road work. You're going to run a mile the first day of practice.' There's a note in the sports section of tonight's paper that says the same thing."

"That slave driver!" Ralph grumbled. "If he had his way, we'd all have been using a pick and shovel this summer. He'll be right pleased with 'farmer boy' Clint here. But he'll hate me."

Ralph's tone got under Clint's skin. "I didn't work in the fields only to get into condition," he snapped. "I can use the money. We weren't all born with silver spoons in our kissers like you."

Ralph laughed, taking no offense.

He drove Walt on home, and as they pulled away from the curb, Clint said, "You don't need to go past my place. Let me off anywhere along here. I'll walk home. My legs feel cramped and I want to get the kinks out of them."

Ralph glanced at him curiously, but said, "Okay, buddy." He pulled up at the next corner and Clint got out. They said good night, and the convertible moved on down the street, its big bright taillights shining redly in the darkness.

Clint's legs were all right. He had wanted an excuse to walk home. His mind was confused and he needed to think. Something was wrong. The whole evening had been a flop. He felt a vague anger, but he didn't know who or what he was angry at. Ralph maybe. He was getting tired of having Ralph tell him that it made no difference whether *he* won or lost. Ralph himself hated to lose, whether it was football or ping-pong.

And he was thinking of Jeff Washington. He had never paid Jeff much attention. Jeff and his sister Leona had been the only Negroes in high school last year. But there were fifteen hundred boys and girls in Monroe High, and if you wanted to get lost in the crowd, it wasn't hard to do.

He didn't even know where Jeff lived. But he supposed it was across the tracks on the north side of town. In Monroe the north side was the wrong side of the tracks. He knew that Jeff's father was a cleaning man at the First Security Bank. Everyone knew that, because Henry Washington was a college graduate and people liked to say that he certainly didn't need a diploma to push a mop, and polish brass, and wield a dust rag.

When he reached home, he sat on the front steps. After days like this one, his upstairs room stayed hot until midnight or after. But out here it was nice. The night was now sweetly cool. The stars were brilliant and the crickets were fiddling away like mad. He liked these summer nights, and there wouldn't be many more of them.

CHAPTER TWO

Summer was still with them on the first day of football practice. Down in the basement dressing room, under the gym, it was pleasantly cool. But outside a blanket of heat lay over the city. Clint Thomas felt fine. In his mind, the summer was past. It had ended Friday night with the state swimming meet. Now he could forget swimming and farm work and all the other activities of vacation time, and concentrate on football. He liked the fresh feeling that came with the start of a new football season.

He had redeemed himself somewhat, in his own estimation, by taking second place in the backstroke at the state meet. Monroe had taken third place, which wasn't bad at all, considering that eight teams had competed. Judy had been largely responsible for Monroe's showing, winning three first places in the girls' events. True to predictions, she had been the outstanding swimmer. She had bettered the state record in the 100-yard freestyle, and again in the 440 freestyle. And she had come within an ace of bettering the record for the 160-yard medley.

Yes, summer was gone so far as Clint was concerned. It would not be long before the leaves would begin to turn and the days would be misty gold and cool.

Clint sat on the bench lacing his football shoes. There was a lot of horseplay and laughter in the room. The noise echoed hollowly from the concrete walls. Harry Diamond, who had worked in the office of his father's lumber yard during the summer, got a laugh when he looked unhappily at Clint and asked, "Do you think the coach really meant it when he said we'd have to run a mile today?"

Clint looked at the dark-skinned boy and chuckled. "You can depend on it, Harry. Sully isn't the kind that wastes words."

Harry assumed an attitude of total exhaustion. His shoulders slouched and his tongue hung out. "I'll never make it."

Archie Strong, burly, redheaded and freckled, marched over and stood before Harry. Archie had worked for the forest service all summer. He was bare to the waist. With much aplomb and affectation he displayed his work-hardened muscles by posing like a muscle man. Archie weighed one-ninety, and he put on quite a show.

He looked around at them. "Been rasslin' cougars and b'ars all summer," he said. "It's going to be mighty ha-a-a-rd to settle down and not play too rough with you boys."

Harry looked at the first-string guard with mock admiration and awe. "You great big hunk of beautiful man!" he said. Then suddenly his right arm flashed out and his fist plunked into Archie's bare stomach. Archie grunted with surprise.

"Soft as butter," Harry declared. "Bet you didn't do anything in the hills but sit on a stool in a lookout station."

The redhead grinned at him and made a face and went back to his locker.

Walt Tracy spoke up in a confident tone. "I'm ready. I've been jogging the streets every night for the last ten days."

Clint glanced across the room at Ralph. Ralph was pulling on a white cotton practice jersey, marked with grass stains, although it was freshly laundered. When his head popped through the opening, his eye caught Clint's and he grinned and winked. The old self-assurance was there. Clint had to laugh. Unless he was superhuman, that mile run was going to half kill Ralph. But evidently he wasn't worrying.

They walked out to the practice field in groups of two and three. Clint walked with Harry Diamond and Ralph. Over to their right, the brick school buildings lay quiet in the hard, bright sunshine. It was still a week before school would start.

The practice field was in excellent condition. The

turf was thick and green, like a carpet. With thirty pairs of cleated shoes running around on it, it would not stay that way long.

They tossed a ball around for a while, getting the feel of the pigskin again. Then some of the fellows began kicking. The smack of toe against football sounded cleanly through the afternoon air. Clint loped around, exchanging passes with Ralph. His muscles felt loose and strong.

When Coach Leon Sullivan and his assistant, Jack Tucker, showed up, the boys quit playing and gathered around. There were handshakes, and Sully had a few words for each of them.

"You've grown," he said to Clint. "Look fit, too."

Clint grinned. "You don't look soft yourself."

The coach was a stocky man, with hair beginning to gray at the temples, and keenly observant eyes. He walked with the balanced, graceful movement of a long-time athlete. He could be soft and he could be tough. Now he suddenly quit smiling and said, "All right, let's get to work! Line up for calisthenics."

The coach didn't bear down too hard, but it didn't take much to make the sweat pour. After the drill, he put the backs to work running back punts, while the linemen charged down on them. But there was no tackling. It looked like an easy practice, except for that mile run coming up.

After an hour of practice, Sullivan blew a blast on his whistle and yelled, "All right, everyone take four laps around the track! Anybody who doesn't make it tonight tries again tomorrow, and the next day, and the next day. Let's go!"

Thirty pairs of cleated shoes crunched in the cinders of the track that surrounded the field. A few eager boys took the lead, setting a fast pace. It was a temptation to take off after them, but Clint settled down to a steady gait, breathing deeply, carrying his arms low.

The first lap wasn't bad. The second was a little tougher. On the third lap the heat and the effort began to exact its toll. The quick starters had now fallen back. The squad was strung out, with some stragglers way back. The coaches kept yelling at them, urging them on. "Get the lead out! Let's go—let's go!"

Clint was among the leaders, and he intended to stay there. He was tired of being an also-ran. The run had taken on the aspects of a race. Archie Strong was on one side of him and Walt Tracy on the other.

"Been——climbin'——mountains——all summer," Archie said between gusts of breathing. "This is——a piece——of cake."

Clint made no reply. He was saving his wind. He was panting now, and he felt the sweat streaming down his sides and his pulse hammering in his temples. Pound —pound—pound! He wanted to slow down, but his pride drove him on. He kept his head down, not wanting to see how far he had to go. He was beginning to get a pain in his side. Hang it, where was the finish line!

The coaches stood at the imaginary finish line. Clint

called on his reserves for a sprint. To his surprise, his body responded like a good car when you tromp on the accelerator. He beat Archie and Walt by a half-dozen steps. He left the track and flopped on the ground and sat there and panted and blowed. "It feels good to come in first for a change," he thought, thinking of the swimming races.

Half the squad had slowed down until they were moving at a pace scarcely faster than a shuffling walk.

"Who's that guy way back?" Archie asked. "He'll never make it."

Clint recognized the creeping figure. "That's Ralph. And I'm not surprised."

Clint sat there while his breathing slowly stilled. Then he and Archie and Walt got up and headed for the showers. They were undressed when the others came slogging in. Clint looked them over. "Where's Ralph?" he asked.

Harry Diamond laughed. "The speed he was traveling, he'll need a lantern to find his way to the dressing room. What's that boy been doing all summer, anyway?"

Clint grinned. "Training on milk shakes and riding in his car. He'll learn."

When Ralph dragged himself in, he was the butt of some good-natured ridicule. He just rubbed his long nose and grinned.

"Did you make it?" Clint asked.

"Naw. I wanted to walk the last half lap, but Sully

said that didn't count." He shrugged. "Oh, well, there's always *mañana*."

The two coaches came into the room and Sullivan called for attention. Silence settled over the room as they stopped what they were doing and listened.

The coach's voice was full and strong, developed by years of shouting, scolding and cajoling on the football field. "Now, most of you know what I stand for," he said. "But there are some newcomers among you, and for them I'll repeat my philosophy. I believe in hard work and teamwork. Football is a game to be played with spirit. Some of you are going to think I'm too tough. I don't think I am. My job is to send you into a game prepared to win, and able to take care of yourselves in any situation. I don't know any easy way to do that. Football isn't that kind of game. If any of you try to loaf, you're going to find that it doesn't work.

"Now, as for training. You need a good night's sleep every night. Nine hours is the minimum. Get to bed by ten. Saturday night will be an exception, but even then don't stay out until all hours. No smoking, no drinking, and lay off the sweets. Football isn't easy, but it has rewards. Some of the rewards concern values that may not be clear to you at the present time. This game teaches you to keep on plugging, sometimes in the face of almost certain defeat. It teaches you to win with modesty, and take defeat without whining. You'll learn that, in spite of what the scoreboard may say, you're never really licked until you quit trying. Those lessons will stay with you. And, believe me, you'll be able to use them later on, this world being what it is.

"One more thing: if you've got troubles or gripes, come to my office and we'll talk them out. Anything I hate is for a player to go moping around with something on his mind, and keeping it all to himself. Get it off your chest and you'll feel better." The coach's rugged face broke into a smile. "This is the only speech you'll get all season, so don't look so solemn."

They laughed then, and the normal noise of the dressing room resumed. After he showered and dressed, Clint said to Ralph, "I'm going in to see the coach. Wait for me, if I'm not out by the time you're dressed."

Ralph, dripping from the shower, gave him a slow smile. "What's the matter? Got problems already?"

"Nope," Clint replied, and headed for the office.

It was a cubbyhole of a place, just off the equipment room. Framed photographs of football teams lined the walls. The coach sat at a desk that looked as if it dated back to pioneer days.

"What can I do for you, Clint?" he asked.

Clint told him about Paul Slansky. "He was strong as a horse in the hayfields, and yet he wasn't clumsy," Clint said. "I think he'd turn out if someone would take him home after practice."

The coach tapped a pencil on the glass top of the desk. "You've got a car, haven't you, Clint?"

Clint hunched one shoulder and grinned. "I guess you could call it that. Anyway, it runs."

[26]

"Could you see to it that this fellow gets home after practice?"

Clint hesitated, thinking of the gas and oil it would take.

"Don't worry about the cost," the coach said at once. "I'll see that you get an allowance for gas and oil. It will come from the athletic fund."

"Sure, I can do it," Clint said, then.

"Fine." Coach Sullivan smiled. "We'll see how good this discovery of yours is."

"If he'll turn out. He's the kind that can be stubborn if he wants to. I'll have Ralph run me out right now, and ask him."

"What's the matter with Ralph, anyway? Has he been lying in a hammock all summer?"

"Just about. But you know Ralph, Coach. He can't get down to business until the pressure is on. He'll snap out of it."

"He'll have to! That boy has a lot of natural ability. But sometimes that isn't enough."

Clint turned to go, but a word from the coach halted him. He swung back. "As long as you're digging up new talent, Clint, how about talking with Jeff Washington? I talk to him every year about this time, but never get anywhere."

Clint frowned. "I saw Jeff about a week ago. Walt asked him if he was coming out, and he said he wasn't. It seems to me that if the guy doesn't want to play, that's his business."

The coach looked into Clint's eyes. "I've heard a rumor that the Washingtons have been looking for a house to buy in a white neighborhood. Have you heard about that?"

Clint shook his head. "No."

"If the rumor is true, Jeff is liable to become pretty unpopular with some people. You're not one of the fellows who would give Jeff the treatment because of that, are you, Clint?"

"No–o–o."

"Suppose the Washingtons bought a house in one of the more fashionable white neighborhoods. Would you still be friendly with Jeff?"

Clint fidgeted. He didn't want to get into any argument with the coach. "I don't know. I haven't given the question any thought. I'll ask him to play, if you want me to."

"Good! You know, Clint, you're a steady boy. I depend on you."

"Yeah, old slow and steady—that's me."

"You weren't so slow in that mile run today."

Clint felt a warm glow of pride. "I'll wake up one of these days and show everybody."

Ralph wasn't in the dressing room, so Clint went outside and found him lounging in the convertible. Clint climbed into the seat. "How about running me out to the river?"

"My, my. First you go to see the coach with some deep, dark problem, and now you want to go to the river. Believe me, buddy, suicide is not the answer."

Clint grinned. "You're real funny today." Ralph started the motor and they rolled down the paved street.

"I'm going to try and dig up some new football talent," Clint said. "This fellow we're going to see is a fullback."

Ralph nodded. "We could use a good fullback."

"Yeah." Last year they had lost every game but one. The main reason had been that they were weak in the backfield. They had no one who could really hit the line. Their offense had been built around Ralph, who was at his best in broken field. They hadn't been able to mix up their plays enough to keep the defense guessing.

The late afternoon sun was hot as they left town and headed into the country. Combines were moving over wheat fields as they passed, and the smell of grain and straw was in the air.

A lane, an open gate, and a rural mail box marked the entrance to the Slansky farm. Ralph raised a cloud of dust as he sped down the lane. He narrowly missed a squawking hen. He braked to a stop in the barnyard.

The Slansky place wasn't much to look at. The house was old and unpainted. It was surrounded by a staggering picket fence. Half a dozen children stood at the fence and stared at the shining car in big-eyed wonder.

"What a dump!" Ralph said.

"Don't talk so loud. Someone might hear you."

Ralph shrugged as if to say that he didn't care.

Clint got out and started for the back of the house. But Mrs. Slansky evidently saw him coming, for she met him at the doorway.

"Hello, Mrs. Slansky," Clint said.

Her broad face was wreathed in smiles. "Hello, Clint."

"Is Paul around?"

Her voice carried a heavy accent. "He down to river with friend. I think maybe he swimming."

"Thanks, Mrs. Slansky. We'll find him."

Ralph and Clint cut across the barnyard. They crossed a small pasture where three milk cows and several calves grazed. The cattle were sleek and fat. Then the boys crawled through a barbed-wire fence and strode into the group of big trees that bordered the river.

They emerged on the river bank. The river was low at this time of year and sand bars and hummocks of gravel were exposed in the river bed. But before them was a pool that was deep and wide. The branches of the trees broke up the hot sunshine and made blue shadow patterns on the water. Across the pool was a sand bar. Two boys were stretched out face down on the sand. Clint was surprised to see that one of them was Jeff.

"Hey, Paul!" Clint called.

The two boys raised their heads and looked. "Hi, Clint," Paul called back.

[30]

"I want to talk with you," Clint said.

Paul grinned. "Well, come on over."

"I've had my exercise for today."

Paul got to his feet, but Jeff remained lying in the sand. Paul dived into the water and swam toward them. He waded through the shallow water at the pool's edge and stood before them. He was a sturdy, straw-haired youth of seventeen or eighteen with pale blue eyes like the August sky. Clint introduced him to Ralph. Ralph acknowledged the introduction in his usual friendly manner. Clint got down to business and told Paul of Sullivan's proposition.

"We can sure use you on the team," Clint concluded, earnestly.

Paul's face was sober and thoughtful. He bent over, picked up a stone, tossed it into the pool.

"Well," he said finally, "I'm sure tempted. I like football. I planned to work on Saturdays this fall, but I guess I can get along without the money. But I start working in the grain tomorrow. I won't be able to turn out until the first day of school."

"That's all right. A few of the guys with summer jobs are still working." Clint laughed and slapped Paul on the back. "I didn't know it was going to be this easy to talk you into it."

Paul smiled. "When a fellow wants to do something anyway, it's not hard to talk him into it."

Clint looked toward Jeff. "I didn't know you knew Jeff."

"Jeff and I are good friends. He's come out here all during the summer to swim. I met him down here on the river the first time."

"How does he get out here?"

"Rides his bike."

Clint whistled softly. "He sure must like to swim to ride a bike ten miles for the privilege. How come he doesn't go swimming at the pool in town?"

Paul's eyes moved around for a moment and then fastened on Clint's. There was a cool anger in Paul's eyes, and a kind of accusing gleam. "He tried that a couple of times. But some 'I-am-better-than-you' hypocrite protested to the manager. The manager didn't say anything to Jeff, but he heard about the protest. And since Jeff doesn't like to go where he isn't wanted, he never went back to the pool."

Clint smiled uncertainly. "Well, don't look at me like that. I didn't turn in the protest."

Paul lowered his eyes. "Sorry. I didn't mean that you did."

"I wasn't the one, either," Ralph put in. After a moment, he added, "But I could have been."

They looked at Ralph. His chin was up in a defiant way, and his eyes were hard.

"You really mean that, don't you?" Paul said.

"That's right."

"And you play football, too?"

"That's right," Ralph repeated.

"That's good. That's just fine! I'm glad I'm turning out. I'll see you on the football field."

Ralph's dark eyes held an angry warning. "If you want to make something of it, now is as good a time as any."

Paul's hands fisted. Clint waited tensely for the first blow. He wanted to jump between them, but something kept him where he was. The tension piled up. Then suddenly Paul's hands opened. He shook his head slowly. "I'd have to tell Jeff what caused the trouble, and it would just be another hurt for him. I'll accommodate you some other time."

Ralph eyed him without saying anything. Clint tried to think of something to say—anything. He said, "I promised the coach I'd talk to Jeff about turning out, but it doesn't look like this is the time to do it."

"Wouldn't do you any good anyway," Paul declared. "Maybe I could talk him into it, but I don't think anyone else could."

"Guess we'd better be going," Clint said. "See you Tuesday, Paul."

"All right, Clint."

Before they left, Ralph and Paul shot each other a look as if to say that things were not settled, that neither side was backing down. Clint was confused as he and Ralph walked back toward the farm buildings. Things happened so fast sometimes. In a few minutes after meeting each other, Ralph and Paul had become enemies. No telling how long it would continue. Clint knew that Ralph would not forget the incident.

They did not say a word to each other until they had reached the car. Ralph shot out of the barnyard in a cloud of dust. "So that's the guy you worked with this summer!" Ralph said, as though Clint had done something wrong.

Clint was calm. "You made him mad by what you said."

"Well—a guy like that . . ." Ralph did not finish the thought, but Clint knew what was in his mind. When Paul had called Jeff his friend, he had lowered himself in Ralph's estimation as much as if he had suddenly declared that he came from a family of lunatics.

"The coach is making a mistake in trying to get that Washington to play football," Ralph said. "It would cause trouble."

"No it wouldn't, Ralph. Negroes are accepted in athletics these days. It's very common."

Ralph went on as though he hadn't heard. "We've got to keep those people in their place. A couple of years ago the Washingtons were the only colored family in town. Now there are a half-dozen families. Treat 'em good and they'll soon be coming in in droves. That's what Dad says. You know what happened the other day?"

"No—what?"

"Henry Washington was looking at those new houses

in Dad's project. Someone asked him what he was doing, and he said he was going to buy a place on the south side. Imagine him thinking of buying one of our new houses. If we let a Negro in one of those houses, the price on the others would drop like a rock—if you could sell them at all."

Clint was thoughtful. "The coach told me he had heard that the Washingtons were going to buy on the south side. But I doubt if they move into a fancy neighborhood. I don't think they've got the money."

"Don't fool yourself. They all work and they live poor. I'll bet they've saved a pile." He glanced at Clint. "What do you think about those people wanting to move into white neighborhoods?"

Clint was annoyed. "I don't know the score about this race problem, and I don't much give a hang. Maybe you're just borrowing trouble."

They rode in silence for a while. Then Ralph said, "If that Washington turns out for football, he sure isn't going to get a welcome from me. If we show those people how we feel maybe they'll stay where they belong."

CHAPTER THREE

THE FIRST DAY of school was different from all other days. It was an attitude of mind, like Christmas or Easter. Everybody was more friendly than usual. As Clint pushed his way through the halls between classes, he was greeted with respect and affection. He couldn't help feeling a little important. This year he was a senior.

The warmth of summer still held, and windows in the classrooms were open to the soft summery breezes. Girls wore summer dresses, and boys were in shirt-sleeves. Football practice during the past week had taken pounds off the boys who had not done hard manual labor during the summer. There had been no scrimmage yet, but Clint suspected that there would be this evening.

He had been so busy during the week that he'd half forgotten Paul Slansky. He found that he and Paul were in the same history class. In appearance, it was a different Paul from the one he had known in the hayfields. He looked clean and neat with hair newly cut, and he was dressed in blue jeans and sport shirt. That was one thing about Monroe High. Blue jeans and sport shirts were almost a uniform, and if some of the fellows could not afford to wear more expensive clothes to school, no one knew the difference.

Ralph Vanderpool showed up, rather elegantly, in light gray flannel slacks, white shirt, and red bow tie.

"Man, you couldn't pay me to wear a tie on a day like this!" Archie Strong remarked.

"They probably don't make them big enough to go around that bull neck of yours," Ralph returned calmly.

After classes, in the dressing room, Clint watched the faces for Paul. Pretty soon, he came in, carrying football gear in his arms, a small smile on his broad face.

"Hi, Paul," Clint greeted him.

Paul nodded. "Hello, Clint. Got any idea where locker number fifty-three is?"

"Sure. Mine is fifty. That way."

Paul dumped his gear on the bench, opened the locker door, and began to undress. There were curious looks as Paul peeled off his shirt. When he bent over to unlace his shoes, the muscles of his shoulders and arms bunched under the tanned skin. The fellows were impressed, and Clint was pleased. He had persuaded Paul to turn out, and he felt a personal responsibility for the showing Paul made.

Then Clint noticed Ralph. There was something

close to hatred in Ralph's eyes. As if he felt the force of Ralph's fixed stare, Paul looked up. Their eyes met and held. It was Ralph who looked away first. Clint sucked in his breath. Evidently they were going to be openly hostile. He wondered what would happen on the football field.

Paul looked good in his football uniform. And Clint knew why. The face with its square jaw, sharp blue eyes and close-cropped blond hair was the same kind of face that looked at you from magazine covers and newspaper sport pages during football season. Paul looked the way a football player was supposed to look.

On the field, Clint introduced Paul to the coach. When Paul moved away, Sullivan said, "He looks all right. You can't always tell by looks though. We'll see."

The squad threw balls around and went through calisthenics. Then they were divided into two groups; backs, ends and center in one group, and the remaining linemen in the other. Sullivan worked with the backs and Tucker with the linemen.

Coach Sullivan was dusting off plays they had used the year before, demonstrating, explaining, having them walk through them. The first-string backfield, except for the fullback spot, was the same as last year. Clint was at right half, Ralph at left half, Walt Tracy at quarter. Jim Davis was moved up from the second string to fullback.

A couple of afternoon's practice and they were beginning to look like a functioning backfield. The old thrill of being part of a smooth-working, hard-hitting backfield returned to Clint. They moved with precision to Walt's commands. His voice was sharp and penetrating, a good voice for signals.

Now and then, Sullivan made substitutions. Clint and Ralph went out, and the second-string halfbacks came in. Jim Davis was replaced by Paul. Now they'd have a chance to see how the big fellow handled himself.

It didn't take long to see that Paul was the real thing. He had nice co-ordination and he was fairly fast. He fumbled a couple of Walt's hand-offs, but it was his first day of practice and that was to be expected. Sullivan watched him like a hawk, his head nodding almost imperceptibly with satisfaction.

The coach blew his whistle and called Tucker over with the linemen. Two teams were quickly named, with Clint and Ralph and Jim Davis back on the offensive team. They started scrimmage. Working from the T formation, Walt handed-off and pitched-out to the other backs. It seemed rough to Clint at first. The first time he was tackled, he was jarred right down to his heels. But soon he was warmed up, and so absorbed in strategy that he did not feel the blows.

Paul went in at fullback on the defensive team. Sullivan wouldn't ordinarily have scrimmaged a player on his first day out, but he knew that Paul was hardened. Paul pulled on his helmet and wiped his hands on his jersey.

Walt ripped out the signals. "Ready . . . Set . . .

1——2——3——4!" Walt took the ball from center, faked a hand-off to the fullback, pitched out to Clint. Clint tucked the ball under his arm and punched at the right side of the line. The hole was there and he skipped through. But someone cut him down from the side before he went far into the secondary. Sullivan's whistle shrilled and the ball went back to its starting position.

On the next play, Ralph took a hand-off and headed around right end. Clint threw a block on the defensive left end and rolled to his feet in time to see Ralph turning on the speed as he headed downfield. He shed tacklers from his pants as he outmaneuvered most of the secondary. Paul had cut over, and was now angling toward the scooting ball-carrier with the evident intention of forcing him out of bounds.

But Ralph was too fast for him. He showed Paul the cleats on his shoes as he easily outran him. Showing off a little, he ran clear to the goal line, grounded the ball, and came trotting back. He lifted his knees high and there was a proud and pleased grin on his face. Clint could read his thoughts. Ralph had discovered that he was faster than the newcomer—that he was still the fastest man on the squad when he was in condition.

Walt called a pass play. He grabbed the ball from center, back-pedaled five paces, cocked his arm and faked a pass to Clint, who was the man-in-motion to the left. The right end had gone down and cut in and Walt rifled the pass. The twisting, speeding ball went right into the end's hands, but he couldn't hold onto it. He dropped the ball.

"You shoulda had that!" Sullivan bawled at the end in exasperation.

But Clint sympathized with the end. Walt's passes were fast and stinging and hard to hang onto. The fellow was accurate, and he could heave long ones or short ones. But he simply didn't have the knack of making them easy to handle, especially the short ones. They had lost games last year because no one could be depended upon to handle Walt's pitches. Clint had taken over part of the passing duties, but he didn't have the throwing arm that Walt had.

They huddled, Sullivan named a play, they fanned into position. Ralph hit the left side of the line and found a hole as big as a highway prepared by Archie. He tore into the secondary at full speed. It looked for a moment as if he might get away again. But Paul charged and hit him head-on. Ralph grunted and went down as if he'd been hit by a truck. When he got up he threw Paul a dirty look and muttered something under his breath. Paul's face wore a little smile. Clint smelled trouble. There had been spite in Paul's tackle. Clint saw Sullivan looking at Paul with a question in his eyes. But this was a game in which a player was not scolded for being overzealous.

Ralph's face was still grim and tight-lipped when the coach blew his whistle and said, "That's enough for tonight. Everybody inside!"

[41]

"Wait a minute!" Ralph said.

Sullivan swung around and stared, dumbfounded at Ralph's tone of voice. Under the coach's gaze, Ralph's face lost some of its arrogance. But his voice was demanding. "How about the guys out for the first time today? Don't they have to take four laps around the track like the rest of us did?"

The coach said nothing for a long moment. Then he turned his head and said, "All right, you new men hit the track. Four laps! Everybody else in." He nodded curtly at Ralph. "You stay. I want to talk with you."

Clint was nearly out of his uniform when Ralph came into the dressing room. His face was sulky, and he threw his helmet into his locker with spiteful force. Clint walked over to him.

"Get a bawling out?"

"Yeah. The old coot asked me who I thought was running the team—me or him." Ralph's tone was bitter. "The rest of us had to run that mile. No reason why the new guys shouldn't."

"I think Sully forgot. And I don't think he'd have minded you speaking up. But you practically yelled at him. He won't take that."

Ralph bent over and stuck out his arms and Clint pulled his sweaty jersey over his head.

"What's gotten into you, Ralph?" Clint asked. "Seems like you're gettin' riled up all the time these days."

"Things seem to be getting off to a bad start this

year," Ralph grumbled. "I'm eighteen years old now. I don't feel like taking the guff that I used to. We're going to be out of high school next spring, and then we're considered grown-up. Old enough to go into the Army and things like that. So, I feel different. And I'm not going to take too much from Sullivan, or anybody else."

"You get tough with Sully and he'll boot you off the squad."

"I'm the fastest man on the squad," Ralph said complacently. "He likes to win games. He won't kick me off."

Clint went back to his locker. Archie jerked his head toward Ralph and said, low-voiced, "What's eating him, anyway?"

"I guess he's feeling sort of grown-up," Clint replied. "That's all."

Paul came in, wet and winded. Clint waited for him to undress so that they could shower together, and then drive home. He asked if Jeff had decided to turn out, hoping he had, not wanting to talk to Jeff himself as he had promised Sullivan.

"I asked Jeff about it," Paul said, "but he's still undecided."

"Looks to me like he's playing hard to get," Clint said.

Paul shot him a look. "I wouldn't say that. Maybe he's got reasons for feeling like he does."

Clint had been under the shower a couple of minutes when Archie came by, grabbed the handles, and turned off the hot water and turned on the cold. Then he seized Clint and held him under the frigid spray. Clint roared and struggled, but Archie's huge arms held him helpless. When Archie let go, he was tingling all over. They went into the dressing room together, laughing and clowning.

It took little more than a half hour to drive Paul home and get back to town. He walked into the house just as his father and mother were sitting down at the dinner table.

He ate slowly, telling his parents about the day's happenings. His father was always interested in how practice had gone, and Clint told him about the trouble brewing between Ralph and Paul.

"I'm afraid that if Jeff decides to turn out there'll be real trouble," Clint said. "Not because he will be playing football, but because there's a rumor going around that the Washingtons are going to buy a house, and that Henry Washington has been shopping around on this side of town. Ralph's got friends on the squad and they might raise a fuss just to show how they feel about Henry looking for a house in a white neighborhood."

"Suppose Jeff wants to play anyway," his father said quietly. "Whose side are you going to be on?"

Clint was evasive. "If it's going to cause trouble—"

"But if he wants to play, he's got as much right as anyone, regardless of trouble, hasn't he?" George Thomas demanded.

[44]

Clint shrugged. "I guess he has." Clint knew his father's attitude in such matters, and it would be useless to argue with him. His father was always talking about fair play. Clint believed in fair play, too. But sometimes things were so complicated that you weren't sure what was fair. The matter confused him, and he didn't like to think about it.

After dinner he had an idea; in fact, a couple of ideas. First, he decided that he'd go and see Jeff as he had promised. He wanted to get it over with. The second idea was more pleasant: he would drive over to Judy's and ask her to go along. He didn't know where the Washingtons lived and he could ask Judy if she knew. He didn't really need an excuse, but it would be easier this way.

He wondered how Judy felt about Negroes. Perhaps she wouldn't want to go with him. Though he could not picture Judy being like that.

When he braked to a stop in front of the Harlin home, he felt a little ashamed of his old Chev. He wished he had a slick convertible like Ralph's. He was nervous. Just because she was friendly that did not mean she really liked him. He'd feel a fool if she turned him down.

Judy answered the door. "Hi!" she said, smiling. "Come on in."

They walked into the living room. He greeted her parents and younger sister, Debby, and sat down on the edge of the davenport. He clasped his hands tightly. He was uneasy about mentioning the Washingtons, but there was no alternative now.

Her face lost none of its pleasantness. "Yes, I know where they live," she said, answering his question. "What do you want to see Jeff about?"

"I'm going to ask him to come out for football."

"That's a good idea!" she said. "Maybe he'd help the team. I want something to cheer about this year. Last year—" She smiled and shook her head.

He grinned. "We're going to have a better team this year. You'll see."

"Well, I didn't mean—"

"It's all right. We were lousy last year. That's no secret." He cleared his throat. "Would you like to go over to Jeff's with me?"

"Sure. I can visit with Leona."

"Okay." Clint looked at Mr. and Mrs. Harlin, but their faces showed no signs of disapproval.

Mrs. Harlin said, "Mrs. Washington has done housework for me a number of times. She's a nice lady."

They drove across town in the long shadows of early evening. They passed through a forlorn neighborhood of shabby, run-down houses, and Clint expected Judy to point out one of them. But they went on. The houses became scattered and few. At last she pointed to a place ahead. "That's it."

It was another shack, painted brown, but the lawn in front was mowed and clean. When they got out of the car, Clint saw Jeff and a colored man in a field that adjoined the lawn. The field was overgrown with weeds, except for a bare strip down the middle. The boy and the man were passing a football back and forth.

"I imagine that's Jeff's dad," Clint said. "I'll go over and talk with them."

"I'll go in and visit with Leona," Judy said.

"You're going inside?"

"Why not?" she asked, eyeing him.

He shrugged. "No reason."

Judy walked toward the house, where somebody was looking out through the glass in the front door, and Clint crossed the lawn toward the field. They stopped playing as he neared and stood and watched him. He greeted Jeff, and then the man came over and Jeff introduced his father. The big man smiled and gave Clint a hard grip.

"I see you still know how to handle a football," Clint said.

Mr. Washington turned the ball over in his large hands. "I always get football fever about this time of year."

Clint grinned. "Could you give some of that fever to Jeff? We'd like him to come out for the team."

The man's face was suddenly solemn. "I'd like to see Jeff play football. I think he's got ability, and he's missing a lot of fun. We've talked it over every year, but it's Jeff's decision to make." He took out a pocket watch and glanced at it. "I've got to be heading for work. Nice meeting you, Clint. I'm always glad to meet Jeff's friends."

Clint felt like a hypocrite. "Thanks—Mr. Washington."

Henry Washington flipped the ball to his son and headed across the lot. Their eyes followed him for a moment. "I guess he was a great football player," Clint said.

Jeff nodded. "Pop was one of the best."

Clint scuffed his toe in the dirt. He was vaguely embarrassed. "I'm not going to give you any sales talk about coming out for football, Jeff. The coach would like to have you, and so would a lot of the fellows. Paul Slansky turned out today. He looks like he might be a real player."

Jeff looked at Clint for a moment, and then looked away. "Paul is a nice guy. I'd like to play ball with Paul."

Clint could feel the chasm between them. But he began to understand that he'd have to meet Jeff halfway to get anywhere with him. Jeff probably understood that Clint had not come to see him of his own accord. Clint felt guilty. He spoke in a different tone. "If you'll tell me what's holding you back, Jeff, maybe we can talk it out."

Jeff fingered the football and said nothing. Clint noticed that his long, big-knuckled fingers went far around the ball. "Well, if you'd rather not talk about it—" Clint said.

Jeff shrugged his broad shoulders. "No, I don't mind telling you how I feel, Clint. Look at my dad. He was a star in college football, and he made good grades in his studies. Then we came up here to live because Leona had a sick spell and we had to get her away from that smog in Los Angeles. And what kind of job does my dad have to take? He's got to be a cleaning man." Jeff gave his head a quick, angry shake. "Why, he could hold down any kind of job—any job at all!"

Clint could read the bitterness in Jeff's face. "I agree with you. That's not right," Clint said slowly. "But what has that got to do with your not playing football? You're not going to help your dad, or yourself either, by just standing on the sidelines."

"I know somethin' about football, even though I never turned out at school," Jeff replied. "Pop has told me things, and on Saturdays some of us play a little football here on this lot. Football is hard work, isn't it? You turn out for the team, and you practice every afternoon. I've watched practice. You get hit plenty hard. Those linemen grunt and strain on every play. Then, you can't stay out late nights. You give up a lot of free time. What do you do it for?"

Clint thought for a long moment, searching his mind for an honest answer. "I guess there isn't just any one reason," he said then. "You just like to be part of something, and maybe you like those cheers on Saturday afternoons and all those people watching you, and you like the way the kids treat you at school because you're a football player. Then there's the competition. Makes you feel alive. Put it all together and it's something that's fun to do."

"You left out something, Clint. You got to feel right about things to play football for a school. You got to be willing to work hard, and play to win. Well, I don't feel right about things. I don't like the way my dad is treated. That isn't all. Suppose I play football. Sure, that makes me more popular with the kids at school. Maybe I even go on to college and be a big shot like Pop was. So I get a diploma and come back here to Monroe and look for a job, and they want to put a shovel or a mop in my hand. You don't need a college education for those jobs." He raised his shoulders. "What's the use?"

Clint was embarrassed again. "I see what you mean. I don't blame you. But you talk like things are never going to change."

Jeff's voice carried a frustrated tone. "Things change —sure. But a lot slower than most people think. Colored boys play on teams everywhere but in the South, so people pat themselves on the back and say, 'Heck, this race problem is all settled.' Then they relax. But you can't just relax. Things aren't right, and they won't be for a long time. How about people who can't get decent jobs because of their race, or can't buy houses where they'd like to live because the section is what they call restricted?"

"You talk about people relaxing," Clint said. "But you're not doing much."

It was a random shot, but Clint saw his words strike home. Jeff grinned self-consciously. He tossed up the football and caught it. He had no answer. Clint pursued his advantage. He pretended indifference.

"I won't argue with you about it. If you don't want to play, that's your business."

Jeff sobered. "I guess a guy can change his mind. I just might turn out. Paul wants me to. And I'm glad you want me to. Nobody ever asked me before except the coach."

"Most of the guys want you to play," Clint said.

"Maybe so. But I know that some of those boys don't like me. Ralph Vanderpool, for instance. Maybe you've heard that we've been thinking about buying a place on the south side. If we do, some people are going to get mad. They'll say that we're forgetting who we are. And people have ways of showing how they feel, whether it's on the football field, or whether you're walking down the street. Ralph and I aren't going to get along if I turn out."

Clint said nothing. Leona and Judy came out of the house. Clint and Jeff walked across the lot toward them. Leona was picking some fall flowers that grew beside the house and arranging them into a bouquet. She glanced up at Clint and smiled and spoke. She was an attractive girl, with large eyes and very white teeth. She picked a few more flowers and handed the bouquet to Judy, who pressed her face to the blossoms.

"Thanks, Leona. They're lovely."

As they rode away from the Washington house, Judy said, "Did you persuade him?"

"He didn't promise, but I have a feeling that he'll turn out."

"Leona is nice," Judy said. "I like her."

"You think it's all right to associate with them?"

"Who's *them?*"

"Jeff and Leona," he said. "Negroes."

She gave him a sharp look. "Sure I think it's all right. Why shouldn't it be all right?"

"You know what I mean. There are lots of people, maybe even the majority, who think that messing around Negroes isn't the right thing to do. They might not admit it, but that's the way they feel."

"I know what you mean, Clint. But I don't feel that way."

At her place they left the car and walked to the front steps. "Sit down a minute," Judy invited.

There was a hint of coolness in the evening air, but the concrete steps held the warmth of the day's sun. From the open door of the house came soft music from a record player.

"It's my record player, but Debby uses it more than I do. I like music, all kinds, don't you?"

"Sure," Clint said.

They sat there, not talking much. Clint looked sideways at Judy. Her cheeks were pink and there were a few sun-bleached, yellow strands in her hair. She hummed softly to the music.

Time passed swiftly, so that it seemed to take only a few minutes for the twilight to change to darkness. A yellow half moon, large and low, hung above the trees. Clint took Judy's hand as he stood up to go.

She walked to the car with him. "Come again, Clint."

He looked into her eyes. "Do you really want me to?"

"I really do."

"Then I'll be seeing you," he said.

CHAPTER FOUR

THE NEXT AFTERNOON, after the last class, Clint headed uneasily for the dressing room. He was both hoping that Jeff would show up, and wondering what would happen if he did.

The place was in an uproar, as usual. Clint and Ralph exchanged wisecracks across the room as they undressed. Ralph was feeling cocky. It showed in the flash of his smile and the confident tilt of his head. In less than two weeks he had worked himself into superb condition.

Clint was pulling on his football pants when Paul and Jeff walked into the room. Voices quit suddenly, and stayed still long enough to make Clint uncomfortable. Paul kept up a stream of small talk while Jeff found his locker, but Clint doubted the boy heard. There was a careful calmness in Jeff's face. Even when someone muttered, "Who let him in?" Jeff's deadpan look never varied. For the first time, Clint understood the courage it took to do what Jeff was doing. On impulse, he called out, "Hi, Jeff! How's the boy?"

"Hello, Clint," Jeff drawled. "I'm okay."

Clint's gesture seemed to restore normalcy to the room, for the fellows returned to the business of putting on shoulder pads, lacing shoes, donning jerseys. Ralph, however, kept staring with obvious dislike at Jeff. Clint watched him narrowly, wondering how long it would be before he thought up something mean to say.

Archie Strong spoke, and his voice was rough. "What're you gazing at, Vanderpool? Ain't you never seen the guy before? Does he fascinate you?"

Ralph's gaze swerved to meet Archie's. After a moment, Ralph made a gesture of contempt with his hand and turned back to his locker. Suddenly Archie jumped up and walked over to where Jeff was undressing.

"Glad to have you with us, Jeff," he said loudly. "It's about time the son of Henry Washington was gettin' into a football uniform."

"Thanks, Arch," Jeff said.

Clint hadn't expected that. If Archie was really for Jeff, it lessened the chances of trouble. Archie was a power in a way that everyone understood—physical strength. He could lick any two fellows on the squad, and everyone knew it. The redhead liked to clown, but he had his serious side, and once he got riled he made people sit up and take notice.

On the field, Sullivan shook Jeff's hand and said, "What position do you play? I may move you later on, but at the start I like to put a boy where he thinks he wants to be."

Jeff held up his hands and spread his fingers. They looked like spokes in a wheel. "I like to catch the ball. I reckon I'll try to be an end."

The coach nodded.

After calisthenics, and a chalk talk in which the coach diagrammed plays on a portable blackboard, Sullivan named two teams for dummy scrimmage. Clint, Ralph, Walt and Paul were in the offensive backfield. Jim Davis' face wore a scowl as he watched Paul move into his place. Evidently Jim was a second-string fullback again.

The offensive team ran plays against the padded defense. The sun beat down and drew water from their straining bodies. It was hard work. But it was no harder than pitching hay, and Clint threw himself into the plays. He was in good shape. It gave him an edge. Maybe this year he would really show them. He inhaled deeply of the grass-scented air as he snapped into position. He felt great.

After a time, Sullivan put Jeff in at right end. In the huddle, the coach explained a pass play to Jeff. They broke from the huddle and trotted into formation. "Let's go, gang!"

The defensive team no longer wore their pads. This was real scrimmage. At the snap signal, Jeff leaped ahead. In ten steps he was under full speed. Walt had faded back to pass. Clint was part of his protective cup of blockers. He threw a block at the defensive right end just as Walt drew back his arm and fired a long one. The ball was leading Jeff, but the colored boy's long legs were moving in a blur of speed. No ordinary player would have caught the ball. But Jeff reached up and plucked it out of the air. He did it easily and efficiently. The coach blew his whistle and called the play back. They ran the same play again, with the same result.

After another ten minutes of scrimmage, during which Jeff snagged every pass within reaching distance of his long arms, the coach took him out.

"Looks like we finally got a ballhawk on the club," Walt said, watching Jeff stroll toward the sideline.

Sullivan didn't say anything, but Clint could see that he was pleased. There were faces on the field, however, that were far from being pleased. Elmer Spang, regular right end, looked toward Jeff with bitterness in his eyes. Elmer had just seen his starting position at right end disappear.

Ralph looked cross, too. But not because he was afraid of the competition. An end did not have the chance to star that a halfback did. Ralph simply didn't want Jeff on the team.

Two nights later, Ralph's pride was rudely shocked. They were scrimmaging. Ralph was at left half on the defensive team, covering Jeff. Walt fired a pass to Jeff and they both reached for the ball. But Jeff's leap was inches higher, and he took the ball with no trouble. He wheeled and headed for pay dirt. Ralph was only three steps behind, but he couldn't catch up. Jeff widened the gap between them at every step, and before he had reached the goal line, Ralph was so far behind that he gave up the chase.

As Ralph trudged back to the scrimmage line, his eyes were gloomy and defeated. He was no longer the fastest man on the squad, and everybody knew it.

As the evenings of practice passed, Sullivan stepped up the tempo in preparation for the first game with Urbana. It seemed to Clint that the coach was always hurrying them just a little faster than they could travel. Practice periods were an involved network of instructions in blocking and tackling, running plays, pass plays, and defense. Under the pressure, tempers occasionally flared. But to almost everyone's surprise, there was no trouble because of Jeff. There had been a kind of awareness on the field for a few days, but it had died a natural death.

There was a small group within the squad, led by Ralph, who never spoke to Jeff. In the dressing room, and even on the field, they pretended ignorance of Jeff's presence. But they did nothing to stir up real trouble. Clint reasoned that they were afraid of the reaction from the rest of the squad if they began saying and doing things.

As for Jeff, he played a cool game. He worked hard on the field, but he gave no indication whatever of getting any enjoyment out of what he was doing. His face nearly always wore a deadpan look, and Clint decided that it was his natural expression. It was plain that Jeff had already learned a lot of football from his father, and what he didn't know, he learned easily. He was intelligent, and a natural athlete. When it came to ball handling, he played with the sureness of a veteran. His only real friend, on and off the field, was Paul. With everyone else, including Clint, he was polite but distant.

It was a good-humored, confident football squad that boarded the bus two weeks later for the first game with Urbana. Clint believed that Monroe had a first-rate team, a well-balanced team with power both in the line and the backfield. But of course you couldn't judge a team before it had been under fire. Today would be a test. Urbana had finished third in conference standing last year and had beaten Monroe unmercifully, 42–6. The Monroe Cougars were out to avenge that defeat, with a hunch that they could do it.

It was fifty miles to Urbana. Clint had an aisle seat beside Ralph. The squad had settled down for the ride and the whine of tires on pavement came through the open windows. The hot weather had worn itself out, but it was a bright day, warm enough so that the air moving through the bus felt good. Ralph didn't have much to say, and spent most of the time staring moodily out the window. Clint wondered what was eating him. Maybe he didn't like it because he was no longer the whole show in the Cougar backfield. Walt had too much to work with now to hand the ball to Ralph every other play.

Maybe, too, Ralph had hoped to be elected captain. After last night's practice, the squad had voted Walt and Archie co-captains. Clint thought the choice had been good. Both boys were football-wise, and one or the other was always on the field.

The bus pulled up outside the stadium at Urbana, and each man lugged his gear to the dressing room under the stands. There was already a sprinkling of fans in the stands and soon they would arrive in force. Clint had seen the caravan of Monroe rooters forming downtown in Monroe. Led by a school bus carrying the Cougar marching band, the procession contained dozens of cars decorated with red-and-white crepe paper streamers and carrying signs that read "Beat Urbana!", and "Make Those Coyotes Howl!".

In the dressing room, Coach Sullivan moved quietly among the players, seeing that ankles were properly taped, joking with players who appeared tense, giving advice, answering questions. Clint watched Jeff, wondering how he was feeling before his first game. Jeff was starting at right end, if Sullivan made no last minute changes. The colored boy seemed completely relaxed, almost sleepy.

They left the dressing room and moved onto the field and the roar that greeted them from the Monroe stands made Clint's blood tingle. The stands were nearly filled, and the air was electric with talk, music and excitement. The brilliant sunshine of the autumn afternoon poured down and glinted from band instruments in the stands and plastic helmets on the field.

During warm-up period, Clint had a few moments to look up into the colorful Monroe stands. He knew that Judy was up there and he wondered where. Last evening they had been in Sam's Malt Shop together and had talked for a long time. Leaving, he had made a date for the movies tonight. He knew that she was watching him and wishing him luck.

Almost before he knew it, Sullivan had them on the sideline and was calling off a list of names. Clint was a starter and he pulled on his helmet. Walt and the Urbana captain were conferring with the officials at midfield. The captain of the Urbana Coyotes wore a flashy yellow jersey with green numerals and green pants. Monroe's captain was garbed in scarlet jersey with white numerals, white pants and helmet. The coin spiraled through the air, glinting in the sunlight. Urbana won the toss and elected to receive.

A silence gripped the crowd as the teams formed for the kickoff. Clint's senses were sharpened to a fine edge as he waited. Slansky, who was kicking, scuffed his cleats impatiently in the turf. Then the referee blew his whistle, its silver note slicing through the air. Slansky's toe connected with the leather, sending it high and spiraling. The red line rolled forward with the roar of the crowd. The game was on!

The Coyote receiver held back, squinting upward

into the sunlight, gauging the descent of the ball. Then he snatched it out of the air and leaped ahead. He picked up interference. Clint avoided an attempted block and almost had his hands on the ball-carrier when another blocker cut between him and his target and slammed him down hard. Clint rolled over and was on his feet in time to see Paul hit the ball-carrier and dump him. The fleet Coyote back had picked up twenty yards. The ball rested squarely on the 35-yard stripe. The stands were alive and noisy.

Working from the T formation, the Coyotes felt out the red-and-white line, slamming into it on three successive tries. They hit off tackle for three yards. A quarterback sneak added three more. Another quick punch at the line gained one. Fourth down and three to go.

There was a lot of pep talk among the red-and-white jerseys as the Coyotes huddled. "Stop 'em cold, gang! . . . Let's go! . . . Block that kick!"

But the yellow jerseys did not go into kick formation. Clint expected another line buck then. But you couldn't be sure. The center bent over the ball. The quarterback ripped out the signals in a shrill, defiant voice. Clint checked the field of play through narrowed eyes.

The quarter grabbed the ball from center, back-pedaled, and cocked his arm. "Pass!" yelled Clint, as he high-tailed it over to cover the racing left end. But the end had the jump on him. He was several yards behind the yellow jersey when the end half turned his body, reached up and snared the pass. With only the safety to pass, he set sail for the goal line. Clint turned on the speed, but he knew that he had little chance to catch the fleeing runner from behind.

Only Walt, the safety man, could stop him. That was what Clint thought until, out of the corner of his eye, he saw Jeff coming in at an angle. Jeff's long legs were eating up the ground at an unbelievable rate. Jeff made the tackle on the 20, hitting the ball-carrier from the side. They skidded and rolled out of bounds together.

As the Cougars moved into defensive positions, the Monroe stands were giving a long, rolling cheer for Washington. Clint watched Jeff turn his head and look at the stands in a kind of pleased bewilderment, as if he found it difficult to believe what his ears were hearing.

Clint knew what Jeff was feeling. He had experienced it himself. The crowd stirred something deep inside you, some half-forgotten thirst for praise and approval. After a time you got used to it and accepted it as part of the game. But a few never lost the deep thrill that the first cheer gave them, and they were the glory seekers. Ralph was one of those.

Action soon drove these thoughts from his mind. The Coyotes, fired-up and touchdown-hungry, went very smartly into formation. The ball was snapped, the quarter spun, faked a pitchout to the right half and then handed-off to the fullback for a simple smash at the line. Archie Strong stopped the fullback cold. On the next play, the Coyote left half swung wide to the right in a sweep. He did a lot of running, but he gained only five yards. The ball was now directly before the goal posts.

The fullback slammed at tackle for three yards. Fourth down and two to go for a first down. The ball was on the 12-yard line. Coming out of the huddle, the yellow jerseys went into place-kick formation. Clint hardly had time to be surprised. It looked as if they were willing to settle for a possible field goal. The quarterback was down on one knee, his eyes on the ball, his closed fists extended. Suddenly his hands flew open. The ball spiraled back, low and fast. The red-and-white line charged.

Quick as a flash the quarterback was on his feet, arm cocked. Clint looked around wildly. Over on his right an Urbana receiver had already sliced into the end zone. He was wide open. The pass traveled like a bullet into his waiting hands, and the Coyotes had scored!

For a space of five seconds the stands were stunned into silence. The trick play had taken them unawares, just as it had the Cougars. Some probably wondered if the play was legal. But the referee's hands were over his head, denoting the touchdown. Suddenly the Urbana rooters went joyously wild. "Boom——boom—— boom!——" went the bass drum. There was an explosion that sounded like a shotgun. The cheerleaders were turning cartwheels. But among the red jerseys on the field, there were head shakings and mutterings. They had been caught flat-footed.

As the teams lined up for the try-for-point, the Cougars were wary. The Coyotes were again in place-kick formation. Would they do the unexpected and try another pass? They didn't. The holder snagged the ball, and the kicker stepped forward and planted his toe into the leather. The ball did not travel far. Archie had bulled his way through the line and shot up his arms. The ball struck him squarely in the face and bounded away.

Archie stood with his face covered by his hands. His teammates gathered about him anxiously. Over on the sideline, Coach Sullivan had stepped onto the field. Then Archie took his hands away. His face was red as fire and a small stream of blood was oozing from one nostril. Tears were trickling from the corners of his eyes. He brushed away the tears with the back of his hand in an angry gesture.

"Well, what are you baboons gawking at!" he snapped. "Let's get on with the game."

They laughed their relief.

As the Cougars waited for Urbana to kick off, Clint swept his eyes around. There were three deep men on the kickoff. He was on the right, Walt was in the middle, and Ralph on the left. Ralph stood with hands on hips, grace and alertness in every line of his lithe body. He was a good back. Clint felt a surge of confidence in his friend. It was hard to doubt him, because he never doubted himself.

The whistle cut through Clint's thoughts. The Coyote kicker was bearing down on the ball, and Clint's muscles tensed. The ball came zooming at them, angling a little to the left. Walt started to drift over, then yelled for Ralph to take it. Ralph fell back, reached up his hands. The leather splatted into his palms. Like a sprinter leaping from the mark, he moved ahead. Clint raced over to help form interference.

A tackler reached for Ralph and Clint threw his body between them and cut the yellow jersey down with a rolling body block. Ralph squirmed and rocketed his way downfield. Speed and deception and timing took him over the chalk stripes. Clint jumped up. He could hear the roar and see the blur of movement as the people in the stands came to their feet. It looked as if Ralph might go all the way. But he skidded on a pivot and one knee touched the ground. He started to run again, but the referee's whistle stopped him. The referee placed the ball on the Coyote 40-yard line.

As they went into the huddle, Clint saw the happy shine in Ralph's eyes and it reminded him of the old days. He felt like saying to Walt, "Give the ball to Ralph. Let him bust this old game wide open."

Walt did give the ball to Ralph. But this time two yellow jerseys filtered through the screen of interference and nailed him six yards behind the line of scrimmage.

On a quick-opener, Clint took a hand-off from Walt and hit the right side of the line. He gained five yards. Then Slansky punched at the middle and made six. "We're rolling, gang," Walt said in the huddle. "Pass 23 on 3. Let's go!"

They snapped into formation. It could be a touch-down pass, Clint thought. They won't be expecting a pass on first and 10. Walt called the signals. At the snap signal, Clint and the two ends raced downfield. Jeff cut in, Clint and the other end kept going. The ball went to Jeff in a long high arc. A yellow jersey was in front of Jeff. The pass was high and the two leaped into the air together. Jeff went higher than the Urbana man, but the ball struck his outstretched fingers and bounced off. Incomplete. Clint let out his breath in a groan. He should have had it! Jeff wore a long face.

"That's all right, fella," Clint said, as he came along-side Jeff. "We all miss sometimes."

Jeff shook his head angrily. "I should've caught it."

There was little time for regrets. On a keep, Walt rolled down the line of scrimmage, cut in suddenly when he found an opening, and got away for ten yards before he was stopped. The Monroe fans were on their feet. This new red team looked unstoppable.

And unstoppable they proved to be. Two plays later they had the ball on the 5-yard line. Walt called the signals sharply and handed-off to Slansky, who went up the middle. Shoulders lowered, legs pumping, Slansky drove into a clawing mass of yellow jerseys. There was a pile-up. When the referee had unscrambled the pile, he shot his arms over his head. "Touchdown!"

There was a brief time in which to thump backs in exultation. Someone threw an arm around Clint's shoulder. He turned and was surprised to see that it was Jeff. No deadpan face now. Jeff's eyes were lighted up and his white teeth shone in his dark face. Clint stared at him wordlessly. And suddenly the happy look faded out of Jeff's face.

"Sorry," he mumbled. "Guess I forgot myself."

Before Clint could say anything, Jeff turned and walked away. Clint considered going after him. But he hesitated too long, and the moment was gone.

"He misunderstood," Clint thought regretfully.

They lined up for the conversion attempt. Walt took the pass from center, hurriedly spotted it. Slansky stepped forward and swung his leg. The yellow jerseys charged, but the red line held and Slansky got off an unhurried kick. The ball split the uprights, turning lazily against the blue of the sky. The score was Monroe 7; Urbana 6.

Urbana received after the Monroe touchdown. Once they had kicked off, the Cougars had their hands full for a while. The Coyotes were fast and tough and smart. They almost made a touchdown, using the old Statue of Liberty play. They had shifted into the single wing back formation, the tailback took the center pass and pulled back his arm to rifle it. The right halfback circled behind him, took the ball from his outstretched hand, and ran wide around left end. Twisting and side-stepping and getting nice blocking, the fleet halfback ran through the whole Cougar team. Only Walt was between the ball-carrier and the goal line. Walt tackled him head on at the Monroe 20.

Then a stubborn Cougar defense dug in and held the Coyotes to eight yards in four tries. Monroe took over on downs. With a devastating demonstration of power, the big red team began a downfield march. Walt didn't call for any fancy stuff. Just straight football, with smashing blocks that opened holes in the Coyote line, and backfield men who ran the defenders crazy. The Coyotes hung on grimly and fought, but they simply didn't have the strength to stop the Cougar drive. Monroe tore off five, ten, and twenty yards at a chunk, and marched eighty-eight yards for a touch-down.

Shortly before the end of the first half, a horn squawked and several red-jerseyed players came running onto the field. Clint's replacement was among them. Moments later he stood on the sideline, chest still heaving and face wet with perspiration. He rinsed out his mouth with water from the dipper, and lifted off his helmet. For twenty-five minutes he had been slammed and battered. But still, he always hated to be taken out.

The gun sounded, ending the first half. The score-board read: Monroe, 14; Urbana, 6. Clint wheeled and headed for the dressing room.

The coach didn't have much to say inside. He pointed

[69]

out a few errors, and gave praise where it was due. Clint was sprawled on the concrete floor. Beside him lay Archie with a wet towel covering his face. The coach tried to joke with Archie about stopping the ball with his face. The muffled reply that came from beneath the towel was unintelligible. Jeff sat on a bench, his face once more settled into its old careful calmness.

Coach Sullivan gave Jeff a playful shove. "You should have snagged that pass, Jeff," he said. "You're trying too hard, boy. Relax. Play them like you do in scrimmage."

Jeff nodded and said nothing.

The second half showed a surprisingly rejuvenated Urbana team. For a time their defense was excellent, their offense sparkling. The crowd thought they might see a close ball game yet, as the two teams fought it out between the 40-yard lines. But gradually the Coyotes ran out of gas. Their defense crumbled before the raging Cougars and Monroe punched over two touchdowns in quick succession in the third quarter.

The second of those touchdowns had brought every fan in the stadium to his feet. Taking the ball on his own twenty, Ralph broke into the clear on an end run. Running fast and gracefully, making it look very easy, he outmaneuvered four would-be tacklers of the secondary, leaving them sprawled and bewildered on the turf, and lit out for the goal line. Clint had blocked out one man and was tearing downfield to take care of the safety. It looked as if Ralph had a cinch until the fastest man on the Coyote team, the same halfback who had nearly scored on the Statue of Liberty play, seemingly came out of nowhere and gave chase.

Ralph scooted away as if he were suddenly jet-propelled, but the Coyote back was just as fast. Only a scant three steps behind, it was a question whether he could gain the inches necessary to lay his hands on Ralph's legs when he launched his tackle. Now a third runner entered the race. And it was plain that Jeff was faster than either of the backs ahead of him. He was soon breathing down the Coyote halfback's neck. Inexperienced though he was, Jeff did not forget himself and clip. He drew abreast the yellow jersey and threw his body in front of him. The halfback turned a complete somersault. Clint took out the safety, and Ralph slowed his gait and trotted into the end zone. Scrappy and swaggering, he grinned from ear to ear as the Monroe fans roared out his name. It had been a close thing, but you wouldn't know it to watch Ralph. He acted as if he had done it all by himself.

The figures on the scoreboard at the final gun were Monroe, 28; Urbana, 6.

The squad was relaxed and talkative riding the bus home in the hazy light of late afternoon. Clint lolled comfortably in his seat. He was content. They had won.

Somewhere, Archie had found a pheasant tailfeather. He folded his handkerchief and tied it around his head and stuck the feather in back, Indian-style. Walt solemnly christened him "Chief Ball-in-the-Face."

Archie's face was a sight. His nose was big and red, and his eyes were swollen to mere slits.

Archie looked across at Clint, raised his palm and said, "How."

Clint chuckled gleefully. "First time I ever saw a redheaded Indian."

"Hair just sunburnt," Archie declared.

Clint thought ahead to his date with Judy. He was picking her up at eight. He felt sorry for some of these guys who didn't have a girl. They didn't know what they were missing.

CHAPTER FIVE

C LINT STOOD before the mirror in his room and combed his hair carefully. At length he was satisfied, and he turned off the light and went downstairs. He wore slacks and a sport coat, with his shirt open at the collar.

His father took his eyes off the TV screen long enough to say, "Hey, don't we look elegant! Do you think the young lady will recognize you, all dressed up like that?"

Clint ignored the question. "How about the car keys, Dad?"

"Don't let him tease you, Clint," his mother said. "You should have seen your father when he first came calling on me. The young fellows were called 'sheiks' in those days, after Rudolph Valentino. They slicked down their hair with oil, and wore sideburns, and went around with their eyes half-closed—"

"I don't think Clint is interested in all that ancient

history," Mr. Thomas interrupted. "You'd better get along, Clint. Don't keep the young lady waiting."

Clint grinned. "How about the keys?" he repeated.

His father reached into his trousers pocket, took out the keys, and tossed them to him.

"Thanks, uh—Sheik," Clint said, with a straight face.

His father looked up at him. Clint hot-footed it for the door. "I'm going—I'm going," he said.

He walked around to the garage, inhaling deeply the cool sweet night air. He backed the family car out of the garage and drove down the street.

Mr. Harlin answered the door chimes and let him into the house. Clint talked with him and Debby for a few minutes. Then Judy came into the room. He stood up. In the lamplight her brown hair was lighted with gold, and she looked clean and fresh as a flower. She seemed taller, somehow, and more sophisticated. Then he realized it was because she had on high-heeled shoes. He hadn't seen her in high heels before. Her full skirt swung about her legs as she walked.

In the car, he said, "You look nice."

Her voice was pleased. "Thank you."

He enjoyed the movie. He liked movies better than TV. Afterward they went to Sam's Malt Shop for a soda. The place was filled. Ralph was there with two other fellows and three girls. Clint and Judy stopped to say hello. Ralph was trying to balance a soda straw on the end of his nose.

Because the place was crowded, Clint and Judy took

a small table for two in the back of the room. They ordered sodas. He was proud to be with Judy. Glancing around the room, he decided that some of the girls were prettier, but there was something special about his girl. Maybe he was prejudiced.

They talked over their drinks, laughing easily, and Judy said, "Have you heard about the Washingtons?"

"No, I haven't heard anything unusual," he said. Then he knew what she was going to say and he said it for her. "They've bought a house!"

She nodded. "I don't know if the deal is closed, but they intend to buy a place in our block. It's down around the corner from us, just across the street from the new Vanderpool housing development."

Clint raised his eyebrows. "Mr. Vanderpool will flip his lid when he hears about it."

"There's nothing he can do to stop them. The Washingtons are buying from the owner, and if the owner is willing to sell to them there's nothing Mr. Vanderpool can do." Judy frowned and said quietly, "Already we've heard that some of the people in the neighborhood are complaining. But we're on the Washingtons' side. The Washingtons have lived here in Monroe for a long time. If they want to buy a house, I think they have as much right as anyone. Isn't that right, Clint?"

He dug ice cream from the bottom of his glass, delaying his answer. "I guess they have," he agreed reluctantly. "But it will cause trouble. Jeff has been accepted on the team. This will stir things up again.

About the only place Ralph and some of those guys see Jeff is on the football field. They'll be rough on Jeff when the word gets around about the house. Darn it," he said, "things are going smooth now. Why don't they let well enough alone, or buy a place on the north side? There are places over there where nobody would object."

Her voice rose a little. "You mean that they should buy a rundown shack somewhere? Why should they? Would you want to put your money into one of those places?"

"I guess not," he admitted. "But I bet there'll be plenty of trouble if they try to move to that neighborhood. And no telling how far it will go. It could ruin everything."

"You mean it could ruin the football team."

"Yeah, I guess that's what I mean."

"The football team isn't everything," she said.

They finished their sodas, and she asked him to take her home. On the way out, Clint stopped to say a few words to Ralph. Judy walked right on past and waited at the door.

Riding home, she suddenly said, "If our neighbors make trouble for the Washingtons, I'm sure going to tell them what I think of them."

He tried to laugh. "You sound awfully serious."

"Oh—you!" she said angrily. "You're just like all the rest."

"What do you mean by that?" he asked sharply.

"I guess I mean that most people think the Washingtons should just stay where they are. It's all right for white people to buy new homes, and get better jobs, and have something to look forward to. But because the Washingtons aren't white they're just supposed to stay where they are. It's not fair."

"I don't care what they do," he said. "If they want to buy a house in your neighborhood, who's going to stop them? There's no law against it, is there?"

"You're being unreasonable. You know as well as I do that people can raise such a fuss that the Washingtons will decide to stay where they are. Something like that happened at the swimming pool last summer. Jeff went swimming in the pool and someone turned in a complaint to the manager. Jeff heard about it and wouldn't come to the pool any more." She paused and added, "Do you know who turned in the complaint?"

"No—who?"

"Mr. Vanderpool."

Clint suddenly remembered Ralph at the river that day, and how angry he had been when Paul had said, "Some 'I-am-better-than-you' hypocrite turned in a complaint."

"So that's why—" Clint said softly.

She looked at him curiously. "What?"

"Oh, nothing. I was just thinking."

Clint pulled up at the curb in front of Judy's home. He turned off the motor, but left the lights burning.

"You might as well know, Clint," she said. "I don't like Ralph. And I know he's your best friend."

Clint said nothing.

"Boys are loyal to one another," she said. "I envy him a little."

"I don't know what to think," Clint muttered. "I'm confused."

Her voice softened. "Maybe you're just tired. You've had a rough day."

She opened the car door and he got out and walked to the house with her. "Thanks for a nice evening," she said.

"Good night, Judy."

Driving home, he was in a reflective mood. And in bed, tired though his body was, he could not sleep. He still did not want to get involved in any controversies because of the Washingtons. He had pictured his last year in high school as rolling along like a song, smooth and easy. But he could see trouble coming, and he realized that the neutral game he would like to play would be impossible. He would have to take sides. You could straddle a fence for a time, but after a while the position could become mighty uncomfortable. If the Washingtons were content to stay where they were, things would be all right.

He guessed he was one of the selfish ones—always thinking of himself. His thoughts became jumbled with drowsiness. The football field danced before his eyes. He saw again the pained expression on Jeff's face when he thought Clint had rebuffed him.

"He misunderstood," Clint muttered sleepily. Soon he was snoring evenly. . . .

It was not too late in the season for thunderstorms, and a good one was brewing when Clint drove Paul home after football practice Monday evening. Huge black clouds were boiling up in the west and a stiff breeze quivered the leaves on the trees.

"Did you hear about the Washingtons?" Clint asked.

"You mean about their buying a house?"

"Yes."

Paul nodded. "I knew that they've wanted to buy a place for some time. They've paid enough rent on that little place they live in to buy it a couple of times. Jeff's dad has saved enough money to make a down payment, and they're anxious to buy."

"Do they know that there'll likely be trouble if they buy that place they want?"

"Yeah. They know. And they're worried. But the house is just what they've been looking for. And the fact that Jeff's playing on the team hasn't caused any trouble has encouraged them."

Clint frowned. "This is different. I talked with Judy on the phone last night, and she said that the people in her block are against it because they're afraid the value of their houses will go down if the Washingtons move in. You know how people act when they think somethin' is going to hurt their pocketbooks. Then, Mr. Vanderpool's new houses are just across the street from that place. You can be darn sure he'll raise a fuss. And he's got influence."

"It's too darn bad about the people in those new

houses, isn't it?" Paul said. "If it wasn't for their prejudice, having the Washingtons for neighbors wouldn't affect the price of their real estate."

"But there *is* prejudice, and they will be affected. You can't blame people for looking after their own interests. Besides, maybe they're afraid the Washingtons will let the place get run-down. You've seen some of the shacks that Negroes live in. They look as if they don't give a hang about anything."

"I admit that," Paul said, after a moment. "But there's usually an explanation. The run-down places are the only ones they can get. And what reason is there to fix up a place when the landlord won't help, and when you have nothing to show for your money except rent receipts?" His voice rose. "You could say that the Slanskys don't give a hang about anything because they live in an old house. But that isn't true. We're buying our place, and we're going to improve it, or tear it down and build a new one."

Clint was embarrassed. "I wasn't thinking about you when I said that about people not keeping up their places."

"I know you weren't. But why not include us? If we were renting, I doubt if we would feel like fixing up that old house. And we'd probably get a reputation for being the 'I-don't-give-a-hang' type. The same thing applies to the Washingtons and a lot of other people. I know the Washingtons well enough to know that they'll take care of their new home."

Lightning began to wink and flitter, and the wind lashed the trees alongside the road. Clint remained silent.

Paul gave his head a quick shake. "This race business really gets me at times. If there has to be prejudice, it looks as if I deserve it more than Jeff. My folks could rightly be called foreigners, but people don't look down on me because of that. Jeff's people have lived in this country as far back as he can trace, and the first ones didn't come here because they wanted to. Jeff's dad is a college graduate and he served in the army for four years during World War II. Now, when he wants to buy a decent house for his family to live in, he's going to run into trouble. If you can't see something crazy about that, then I give up!"

Clint bit back a sharp answer. "I didn't say that they shouldn't be allowed to buy a house."

"Just where do you stand on this question, Clint? Are you for the Washingtons, or against them?"

"It's none of your dang business," Clint said.

"Well, maybe you're right."

Clint's anger melted. "I guess I'm edgy about the thing. I'm confused. I've heard it said by people who can quote figures to prove it, that Negroes commit the biggest percentage of crimes in the cities. I've heard some good arguments in favor of keeping the races apart."

"When people live in slums, the crime rate is high among whites as well as Negroes," Paul said. "If people think that nobody cares about them, they're not going to care about themselves."

They began to drop down the long hill to the river bottom. The treetops along the river were swaying together in the wind, and the sky was blue-black. Big drops of rain began to spatter against the windshield.

"Suppose I was on the Washingtons' side," Clint said. "What could *I* do? People have their ideas and it's hard to change them. 'Specially older people. Sometimes their minds are set—like concrete. They get an idea and you can't blast it out with dynamite."

Paul rubbed his fist along his jaw. "Well, our own attitudes make a difference, sometimes. I think we influence other people more than we realize. Maybe you could influence Ralph, if you took a stand."

Clint snorted. "Ha! Me influence Ralph? You don't know the guy. He's got his own ideas."

"Maybe you underrate yourself. Since we're speaking plainly, I'll tell you something else. You've got it in you to be a much better football player. You'd be a first-rate ball-carrier if you just believed that you were."

Clint didn't know whether to be angry or pleased. "I'm slow. It takes speed to be a ball-carrier."

"You're not so slow. You just lack spirit and fire when you carry the ball. You could be great if you wanted to bad enough." He glanced at Clint. "Do you know that the only time you really catch fire is when you're blocking for another ball-carrier, especially

[82]

Ralph? Then you show what you can do when you really try."

They were in the lane, and then in the barnyard. It was raining hard now. "Why don't you come in until the storm blows over?" Paul asked.

"No, thanks. I'd better get home. The storm won't bother."

"Hope I haven't said anything to make you sore, Clint."

"Naw—it's all right." He didn't know if he was angry or not. Paul opened the car door and made a dash for the house.

The storm reached its full fury as he drove home over the country road. Rain drummed on the top and washed over the windshield. He felt the car sway as blasts of wind struck it broadside. The countryside was vague and shadowy until a vivid flash of lightning illuminated everything with blue light. There was a great crash of thunder and the echoes bounced away across the sky.

Clint remembered how scared he had once been of thunderstorms. As soon as the thunder started to crash, he always dived under the bed. Afterward, he had been ashamed. Now, he thought with pride, he had no fear.

But he wondered if some of that old timidity remained in another form. Was he selling himself short on the football field? The thought annoyed him. He remembered the times Ralph had told him, "You're fine on defense and you can block. But you're no ball-carrier. Let your old buddy Ralph carry the ball."

Clint thought for a while and then, with a sigh, shrugged his troubles from his shoulders. Perhaps Paul just wanted to make him feel good. Anyway, he *was* pretty good. He was varsity right half, wasn't he? No matter how good you were, somebody would always be telling you that you could do better if you just tried harder.

The storm had blown over by the time he reached home. The trees were dripping and the sun was shining. The air was refreshing. He walked around to the back of the house. The kitchen door was open and he could smell potatoes frying. His stomach curled. Man, was he hungry!

The sky was blue as a robin's egg, and the field was dry at practice the next afternoon. Clint felt good. He had almost forgotten the talk he had had with Paul the previous afternoon.

The coaches seemed unusually critical and commanding during scrimmage. Sullivan probably felt they might be cocky and slow down after beating Urbana by such a lopsided score. Whatever the reason, his words carried sting.

Ralph missed two blocking assignments in a row, and Sullivan yelled at him, "What's the matter, Vanderpool? Are you scared of those guys? Aren't you happy unless you're carrying the ball? Let's see you get in there and hit those fellows!"

[84]

Ralph's face darkened. His lips moved as he muttered something under his breath.

On the next play, Ralph took the ball and ran wide to his right. Jeff, who was on the defensive team, ran wide with him. Clint was leading Ralph. He slammed at Jeff with his shoulder. But Jeff was a hard man to block. His big hands shoved Clint aside. A moment later, Clint heard a jarring thump as Jeff tackled Ralph head on. Out of the corner of his eye he saw Ralph go heels over head in the air and land flat on his back.

Clint turned around to see Ralph on the ground, his face contorted. He was gasping for air like a fish out of water as he tried to get the air back into his lungs. Jeff was standing over him, his face a mask of concern. Others hurried over.

Finally Ralph sat up, breathing normally again, and held his head in his hands. Jeff reached down a hand to help Ralph to his feet. "Sorry, fella. I sure didn't mean to—"

Ralph slapped angrily at the offered hand. He got slowly to his feet unaided. He turned and looked Jeff in the face for a moment. Hatred glinted in Ralph's eyes. Without a word he drew back his fist and hit Jeff full in the mouth. Jeff reeled backward from the blow. He put his hand to his mouth. The shock of surprise held and he just stood there.

Then Jeff gave a grunt of sudden rage and lunged forward at his tormentor. But Sullivan was between them in a flash. The big man's face was brick-red.

[85]

"Break it up," he snapped. "Break it up!"

Ralph and Jeff glared at each other. Jeff's chest was heaving and he was trembling a little as he fought for control of himself. Finally, he turned on his heel and walked off by himself. Sullivan faced Ralph. He opened his mouth to speak. His words fell like hammer blows in the stillness.

"I ought to throw you off the team," he said. "I don't mind a player blowing his top once in a while when he's hit hard. It shows he's got spirit. But you hit that boy just because you don't like him. You keep treating him that way and you'll find out what happens when I blow *my* top."

They stared at each other for a long moment, and it was Ralph who looked away first.

Sullivan swung around and raised his voice so that all could hear. "And that goes for the rest of you. I'm playing no favorites on this squad. If Washington gets out of line, I'll bawl him out as quick as anyone else. But I'm going to judge a player by the way he plays ball, and not by the color of his skin, or the way he spells his name, or"—Sullivan paused and looked at Ralph—"how long a nose he's got."

Ordinarily, there would have been snickers at the last remark, but it was so quiet on the field that Clint could hear the cars humming over on the highway. Sullivan waited to let the words sink in. Then he called, "All right, let's get on with it!"

Jeff came trudging back to the line of scrimmage,

[86]

wiping a trickle of blood from a split lip with the back of his hand. Clint couldn't help but feel sorry for him. He looked around, wondering what the others were thinking. But he met only blank stares. Paul was an exception. His jaw was hard and his eyes were like blue ice.

It took three plays to start the teams moving normally again. Sullivan and Tucker bawled at them in exasperation. And when practice was finally over, it was a quiet squad that pulled off sweaty, dirt-stained uniforms in the dressing room. Clint suspected that every man was examining his conscience to decide where his sympathies lay. No one who knew Ralph supposed that he was sorry for what he had done. The question at issue was clear. You either had to sympathize with Ralph or with Jeff. It would be hard to tread middle ground.

Still, a shower was refreshing after a bruising practice. A measure of friendly banter started up again. Clint felt his muscles loosen and relax under the warm flow. Ralph stood next to him.

He gave Clint a warm smile. "I haven't been seeing much of you, buddy," he said above the hiss of the water. "What's the matter?"

Clint shrugged. "I had to study the last two nights."

Ralph winked at him. "Over at Judy Harlin's place?"

"No—at home," Clint said with a small smile. It was hard to resist Ralph's friendly manner.

"What're you doing tonight?"

"Nothing, I guess."

"How about coming over to my place and we'll go downtown and shoot a game of pool?"

"Sullivan catches you guys in a pool hall and he'll kick you off the team," Harry Diamond said.

Ralph made a grimace of disgust. "Sullivan isn't kicking *anybody* off the team. Not a first-stringer, anyway. He wants to win games. After the sorry record we made last year, I'll bet he'd do almost anything to have a winning team. These coaches know which side their bread is buttered on, like anybody else."

Harry shook his head. "That doesn't sound like Sullivan."

Ralph ignored him. He said to Clint, "Well, how about it? Will you be over?"

"All right," Clint agreed. He was pretty certain that Ralph didn't mean it about going to the pool hall. He was just showing off.

CHAPTER SIX

A<small>T TEN MINUTES</small> of seven, Clint left the house and walked down the street toward Ralph's. It occurred to him that he was always going to Ralph's place, instead of Ralph coming to his.

Mrs. Vanderpool let him into the house. She was a white-haired lady, friendly in a quiet sort of way, and usually worried-looking. Clint instinctively liked her. Mr. Vanderpool and Ralph were watching TV.

"Sit down, buddy," Ralph drawled, without taking his eyes from the picture. "Program will be over in a couple of minutes."

Clint took a chair, but instead of watching the TV screen, his eyes wandered about the large, richly-furnished room. Soft lamps shed light on rugs that were deep and colorful. The furniture had an expensive look. The fireplace was huge.

An old painting hung on the opposite wall. Mr. Vanderpool had bought the picture at an art show in the East, and Ralph had said that it cost ten thousand dollars. Clint studied it and decided that it wasn't worth that much.

The program over, the TV was switched off, and Mr. Vanderpool had a few joking words for Clint. He was a big man and he spoke in a booming voice. It wasn't hard to see where Ralph got his pleasant, friendly manner. Clint knew that a lot of people did not like Mr. Vanderpool. They thought he was puffed up with importance. Yet they could not help but have respect for his success, and he was a power in Monroe.

They did not like him, but they said, "Yes, sir!" and "Right away, sir!" and they looked at him with a certain amount of awe. Their attitude confused Clint. Maybe they were a little afraid of him.

Ralph went to his room and came back wearing a sweater. Mr. Vanderpool looked up from his newspaper and said, "Where are you young bucks going tonight?"

Ralph shrugged. "Just downtown, Dad."

"Well, don't stay out too late."

"Sure, Dad."

They went outside, got into the convertible, and drove toward town. Ralph parked the car in front of the Malt Shop, and Clint told himself that he had been right. Ralph wasn't going to the pool hall. He got a surprise then, when Ralph started up the sidewalk. Clint held back.

"Come on," Ralph said impatiently.

"Where are you goin'?"

"To play some pool, like I said. I don't want to park

the car in front of the pool hall. I'm not *asking* for trouble."

So he had meant it, Clint thought. He had a strong desire to tell Ralph to go hang. But habit, or friendship, or something he did not understand, made him choke down the words. "Come on!" Ralph repeated.

Clint walked up the street with him. He wondered why it was so hard for him to say no to Ralph. Maybe it was because Ralph never expected him to say no. Ralph was used to having his own way. That very fact seemed to give him a kind of power over others.

"What if we get caught, Ralph?"

"We won't get caught. It's no fun to play by the rules all the time. That Sullivan thinks he's really somebody. Telling everybody what to do, bawling them out—"

Clint knew that this was Ralph's way of getting even with Sullivan. Ralph had to get back at him some way, even if it was only breaking a training rule.

They walked some fifty yards up the block and then cut into a dimly lit alley. They walked another half block in the alley, the sound of their hard-heeled shoes echoing ringingly from the brick walls on either side. They turned into a back door and entered the Pastime pool hall. The big room was noisy with the sound of clacking pool balls, laughter, talk.

They selected a table at the rear of the room and began to play rotation. Clint had never played much pool and he was no match for Ralph's practiced skill. He was uneasy, too. He kept glancing toward the front of the room. Sullivan was known to check up on his players occasionally.

But Ralph was the very picture of confidence as he calmly chalked his cue and took another shot. Soon Clint forgot his fears and concentrated on the game. He was standing with his back to the front door when a voice came from directly behind him.

"Having a good game, fellows?"

Clint jumped and wheeled around. It wasn't Sullivan—it was Tucker. His face was dead serious. Clint wasn't able to think of anything to say. But Ralph, dark eyes defiant, said, "We were, until you showed up."

Tucker gave his head a shake. "I don't understand why you do things like this. You know that Sully told you guys to stay out of pool halls. What's the matter, don't you like to play football?"

Ralph leaned on his cue stick. "You're not going to blab to Sullivan, are you, Tucker? We're behaving ourselves. We're just having a little fun."

Tucker stared at Ralph for a long moment. "Sometimes you rub me the wrong way, boy. You always seem to think you deserve special treatment. If it wasn't for that, I'd let you off with a warning. As things are, I'm reporting you." He looked at Clint. "I'm surprised at you, Thomas. I thought you had better sense than to pull something like this. I thought you were more grown up. This kind of stunt is kid stuff."

"Now wait a minute—" Ralph began.

"You wait a minute!" Tucker snapped. "You may be able to push some people around—people like Jeff who can't do much about it. But you're not pushing me around. Just remember that, Vanderpool. Now why don't you guys jump out of here."

Ralph took a handful of change from his pocket and laid a coin on the table. He gave, or tried to give, Tucker a contemptuous look. Then he turned on his heel and headed for the door. Clint followed.

Walking up the alley with the cool night air on his hot face, Clint didn't know if he was angry, or just disgusted.

"Well, we sure stuck our foot in it this time," he said.

"Forget it! Sullivan won't do anything."

Clint mimicked Ralph's tone. "Oh, heck no! Sullivan won't do anything. Sullivan is scared to death of us."

Ralph shot him a look. "You gettin' wise?"

Clint spoke quietly, but with emotion. "What makes you so sure? Why are you always so dead certain that nobody can do anything to you? You talk like—like you owned the whole town. Even the whole state!"

They had come to the sidewalk, and they stopped and looked at each other. "You probably blame me for what happened back there," Ralph said. "Well, let me tell you something. You're old enough to make up your own mind. You have no right to blame anybody. If you ask me, you'd let anybody lead you around by the nose, and then blame them if something went wrong."

Clint saw red. He drew back his fist.

"Go ahead—start something!" Ralph taunted him. "You're mad. The truth stings, doesn't it?"

Clint dropped his hands. "I guess there's truth in what you say. I always let you tell me what to do. Maybe I was weak. But no more! I can change. You and I are through. And while I'm in the mood, I'm telling you that I think your hitting Jeff this afternoon was a lousy thing to do. And I don't think you're going to get away with it."

They stood there, their quick, harsh breathing audible. Ralph smiled uncertainly. His voice took on a wheedling tone.

"You're not going to let that Washington guy split us up, are you, Clint? We've been pals for a long time. We've had some good times. We planned on going to college together and playing ball together. Are you going to throw all that away?"

Clint said nothing.

"I shouldn't have said what I did to you. Let's forget it. Let's go up to the Malt Shop and have something to eat. Make us feel better. How about it?"

Clint looked at him, then gave his head a stubborn shake. "I reckon we're through. And I guess this has been coming on for a long time. Maybe, if you start treating Jeff like a human being, and if you stop acting like you're something special, we might be friends again. Until then, we're not friends."

Ralph's manner changed at once. His voice was hard. "All right! If that's the way you want it, it's okay with me. I know that you've been feeling sorry for that Washington all along. You haven't been fooling me, fella. I've gone out of my way to be good to you. And if you think that you and your crummy friends are going to get the best of this argument, you're all wrong. Just you wait and see."

"We can take care of ourselves," Clint said. He turned and walked up the street.

He walked swiftly, pounding his heels against the pavement, for a half mile. Then the deep beat of his anger eased. He began to think clearly, and he felt lighter and lighter, almost happy. Finally he laughed aloud. He felt a strange new freedom. Even if he got the boot by Sullivan, maybe it was for the best. Sometimes it took something serious to straighten a fellow out. When things were going smoothly, he was willing to take things easy. He had to be pushed and stung before he showed his real strength.

The night wind rustled the trees and now and then sent a shower of leaves down on him. He looked up at the stars, unusually bright in the blue-black sky. He promised himself that never again would he lean on anybody. He'd make his own decisions. He'd be his own man.

The next afternoon, Clint sat on the bench in the dressing room, not bothering to undress. He had a feeling of dread that seemed all out of proportion. All day his worry had driven all else from his mind. The prospect of being kicked off the team made him feel sick inside.

He knew how it would be. He had seen it happen before. At first, you got a lot of sympathy. But that passed, and you'd find yourself sitting up in the stands on Saturdays, playing the game vicariously, eating your heart out because you weren't down there. And pretty soon people would forget that you had ever played football. You'd meet football men in the halls and they might speak, but they wouldn't stop. You'd be an outsider. He knew how it would be.

Across the room, Ralph stood leaning against a locker, trying to appear relaxed and careless. But, for once, he fooled no one. His laughter was too brittle, his movements nervous and jerky. Watching him, Clint realized that Ralph was not so tough when the chips were down.

The word had got around. The fellows weren't saying much to them. Archie apparently spoke for the rest when he looked at Clint and said, "You characters must really love to play pool to risk getting the boot for it." He shook his head.

Clint was painfully embarrassed. When Archie put it that way, it made them look like fools.

He was relieved when Sullivan came into the room and called their names. They followed him to the office. Clint was anxious to get it over and done with.

The office seemed stuffy. Sullivan sat at his desk and looked from one face to the other. "Well, boys, what have you got to say for yourselves?"

Ralph lifted his shoulders and let them fall. Clint said, "Nothing, I guess."

Sullivan began to finger a pencil. "I suppose you think I'm an old woman for making a fuss over what you consider to be an innocent game of pool. But I had a good reason for telling you fellows to stay out of pool halls. Four or five years ago, some of my players were approached in that same pool room and offered money to throw a championship game. Their reply was to grab the two men who made the offer and throw them into the street. But there was talk, and it caused a bad situation for a time, and since then I've asked my boys to stay out of pool rooms during football season." He paused and added, "There are much better places to spend your time, anyway."

There was a long silence. "I don't believe you boys meant any harm," Sullivan said then. "Maybe I should explain the reasons for my rules, rather than just hand them out cold. I'm going to forget this incident. Now get back in there and suit up."

They left the office quickly. Clint was so relieved he felt he was floating. He suddenly wanted to laugh. He banged open the door of his locker and took out his uniform. A hand fell on his shoulder. He turned and looked into Paul's pale blue eyes.

"I'm glad you made it, Clint," he said. "I really am."

"Thanks, Paul." He had a sudden inspiration. "Will you do me a favor?"

"Sure."

Clint turned around and bent over from the waist. "Give it a kick, Paul."

Paul hesitated.

"Go ahead!" Clint insisted. "You promised."

With a chuckle, Paul planted his cleated shoe on the target and pushed. It wasn't a kick, but it served the purpose. Clint stumbled forward and fell. He rolled over, sat up, and grinned. "Now I feel better."

Jeff, who was standing nearby, laughed aloud. It was the first time Clint had heard him laugh. Some of the other fellows joined in. But Ralph remained sober.

"I knew he wouldn't get rid of us," Ralph said. "He wants to win games too much for that."

Archie, who was on his way out, stopped and looked at Ralph with distaste. "You're way off the beam, fella. I wonder just how much it will take to wake you up. You give me a pain."

Ralph started to say something, thought better of it, and clamped his mouth shut tight. Archie went on. The others looked at Ralph curiously, and Clint wondered, as Archie had said, "just how much it would take to wake him up."

It rained the night before the Oak Hill game, and they played on a wet field with a slippery ball. Monroe had too much power for Oak Hill and won by a score of 28–7.

The following Saturday was a beautiful October day. The sky was clear, and there was no wind. It was perfect football weather. As Clint rode across town in the school bus to Cougar Bowl, where all the home games were played, he could sense the taut excitement in the air. The game today was with *the* Stratford Bulldogs, conference champions of the year past. Stratford had lost most of its first-stringers through graduation, but they still had a powerful team. Today's game would be Monroe's first real test. The outcome would determine whether the Cougars had a first-rate team, or whether, until now, they had merely lacked competition. Sullivan had driven them unmercifully during the past week's practice in preparation.

Jeff was sitting across the aisle from Clint. His face was melancholy, impassive. Clint wondered what was going on in the fellow's mind. Since his break with Ralph, Clint had made a special effort to be nice to Jeff. He liked him. Jeff was inclined to have moody spells, but he did not take it out on others.

When the red-jerseyed Cougars came out of the dressing room beneath the stands and ran onto the field, precisely thirty minutes before kickoff time, the welcoming roar from the Monroe fans burst upon the sunshiny air like an explosion. The home folks had turned out in force for the game. It was good to get onto the field and move around. Clint still hadn't been able to shed the pre-game jitters.

Towering, booming punts and spiraling passes marked the warm-up. The Cougars gave curious looks at the black-and-orange shirted Bulldogs at the south end of the field. There was exciting band music, and an electric tingle in the air that made every player more than he could ever hope to be on the practice field. The football field, not used until now, was in beautiful condition. The turf was deep and springy under Clint's feet.

Monroe won the toss and elected to receive. The teams moved onto the field. "Ready, Monroe?" Archie Strong waved his arm at the referee's query. "Ready, Stratford?" Stratford's captain signaled that they were ready. The whistle set the black-and-orange jerseys into motion.

"Plunk!" The ball sailed high and far, diagonally downfield to the 10-yard line and into the waiting arms of Ralph. He started up the field fast. Black jerseys went down like bowling pins before Monroe blockers. Clint hit a Stratford man with his shoulder, putting him out of the play without leaving his own feet. Then he headed downfield, looking for more black jerseys. Ralph made a brilliant runback of thirty yards before he was dumped hard on the Monroe 40.

They came out of the huddle on the run, a team with a confident air of knowing what it was about. Clint was alert but relaxed. Tightness always left you after that first play. Walt's signals were clear, crisp, defiant. He spun, faked a hand-off to Ralph, and handed-off to Paul. Paul slanted off tackle and drove up for several yards, then was snowed under.

Next came a surprise play. On an option play, Walt rolled down the line of scrimmage, looking for an opening. But there wasn't any. He faked a pitch-out to Clint. Then he saw Jeff in the clear and jump-passed a low, hard spiral right into his hands. Jeff was dropped immediately, but the play had picked up ten yards.

"Twenty-seven on three!" Walt said in the huddle. "Let's go!"

Clint felt a cool thrill as they snapped into formation. It was his ball. Walt would fake a hand-off to Paul, who would punch into the line. Then Walt would pitch-out to Clint, who would go wide on an end run. It was strange how eager he was to get his hands on the ball. He used to dread it. There was always a chance of fumbling or pulling a boner. It had been easier running interference and letting someone else tote the leather.

But Clint had changed during the past couple of weeks. He had discovered, as Paul had told him, that he could be a better player. And particularly a better ball-carrier. He had learned that if he kept his wits about him and played it cool, he could outsmart most tacklers. His shiftiness made up for a lack of blazing speed. He ran hard and cleverly. He had a good sense of timing.

The ball spatted into his hands. He rode the tail of

his interference as he angled toward the sideline. As he neared it, a black jersey bore down, trying to force him out of bounds. Clint swung his hips and the tackler missed. He cut back in and was in broken field. Side-stepping, changing pace and feinting, he eluded the grasping hands of the tacklers in a way that surprised even himself. Exultation rose in his throat as he aimed straight for that final stripe. Only one man, the safety, between him and pay dirt.

He headed directly for the man, freezing him in his tracks. As the safety launched his tackle, Clint crossed his right leg over his left, planted a stiff-arm on the plastic helmet and shoved hard. The safety went sprawling. Clint was free. He raced over the goal line standing up. The stadium was in an uproar. The sound was music in his ears.

His teammates pounded him on the back. Then they went into formation for the conversion attempt. Paul was in the kicking slot, Walt was holding. The ball was snapped, and Paul put it squarely between the uprights for the extra point. A big, big seven went up on the scoreboard for the Cougars.

As they trudged back to kick off to Stratford, Ralph came alongside. He gave Clint a crooked grin. "Big hero, now," he said. "Get your picture in the paper."

Clint could think of no retort. There had been few words between him and Ralph since that night they had played pool.

The ease with which they had made that first touchdown was misleading. After the kickoff, Stratford hit with speed and deception from the split T. The Bulldogs made a determined drive forward. Monroe retreated doggedly, fighting for every inch, but within a matter of minutes the Bulldogs were on their 5-yard line. The Bulldogs were fired-up and anxious. Too eager, maybe. The quarterback handed-off to the fullback and the plunging fullback bobbled the ball. Harry Diamond sliced through and pounced on it, and the drive was stopped.

The Cougars went into punt formation, Slansky back. A small, favoring breeze had sprung up. Slansky stood with his body slightly bent at the waist, his hands extended at hip height. The pass from center was sharp and true. He kicked the ball out of danger as calmly as if he were on the practice field.

It was a beautiful kick. The breeze helped it along, and the Stratford safety was playing up too close. The ball soared over his head. He chased it frantically, picked it up, wheeled and started to run. But Jeff dumped him before he had taken three steps. The fans on both sides of the field took their seats with audible sighs of relief.

"Yea, Cougars . . . Yea, Cougars . . . Fight— Team—Fight!" came the cheer from the Monroe cheering section.

Again the orange-and-black got a drive under way, and again they were rebuffed as they neared the goal line. With a mere three yards to go for a first down, the

Bulldog fullback went up the middle and didn't get anywhere. Monroe took over on downs on their own 10-yard line.

Dirty, sweating, lost to everything except the game, the red jerseys huddled. There were murmurs of disapproval when Walt called the play. A pass on first down on your own 10? If it didn't work, they would look awfully silly. But it might work. They had been playing conservative football. The Bulldogs wouldn't be expecting a pass. Anyway, Walt was the boss.

Walt got first-rate protection from the rushers, but he danced around, waiting for Jeff to get downfield, and was almost trapped. Then his hand moved forward and the ball spiraled off his fingers in a high, lovely arc. Jeff had raced downfield and then executed a deft buttonhook. The ball settled lightly into his arms. But before he could wheel and get away, two black jerseys fell on him. First and 10 for Monroe on their own 49.

Clint took a hand-off and, legs pounding in savage, driving thrusts, punched into the right side of the line. It seemed that the whole Bulldog team met him at the line of scrimmage and slammed him down and fell on him. He felt the ball leave his hands. He got to his feet slowly, a little shaken up, to see the referee waving his arm toward the Monroe goal. The Bulldogs had recovered. Linesmen moved the chains on the sideline. Clint ripped a handful of grass from the turf and tossed it away in disgust.

A voice at his side said, "Forget it, Clint. We'll stop 'em."

He looked gratefully at Jeff and went to his defensive position. No time for regrets in football. If you stopped to worry about one mistake, you left yourself wide open for another.

The Bulldogs came out of the huddle smartly. There was a man-in-motion on the play. At the snap signal, the quarterback back-pedaled to pass. The left end was racing downfield, and Clint went with him. But the end was running only as a decoy. It was the man-in-motion, the right halfback who had run wide to the left, that took the pass. The halfback was fast and he scooted down the sideline like a greyhound. Clint and Ralph and Walt pounded after him, but it was no use. Walt lunged and made a futile grab at him on the 10. An outstretched hand slapped one of the halfback's shoes, but that was all. He went over the final stripe, and the Stratford fans howled and roared and shouted their approval.

"Block that kick . . . block that kick . . . block that kick—" the Monroe stands chanted, as the teams lined up for the conversion attempt.

The kick was not blocked, but Harry Diamond and Archie charged through and hurried the kicker, and the kick was wide of the uprights to the left. The score was Monroe, 7; Stratford, 6.

The rest of the half was a brutal, seesaw battle that

found neither team able to get into scoring position. The defenses of both had tightened.

As Clint left the field at the end of the half, he was as tired as he had sometimes been at the end of a game. The pressure that a tough, capable team like Stratford exerted really took it out of you.

He spent half of the third quarter sitting on the bench. Coach Sullivan did not believe in playing his regulars a full game unless he absolutely had to. Clint was impatient to get back in. The Cougars and the Bulldogs were slugging it out between the 30-yard lines. Jeff was the key man on the red team. He was playing a cool but ferocious game. He played almost with desperation, as though it were the last game he would ever perform. It was almost impossible to block him out of a play, and he seemed incapable of making mistakes on offense. On passes, he usually managed to outsmart the defense man with his deceptive speed. When he caught a pass, the ball seemed to settle lightly into his hands, although it actually traveled hard and fast.

Now, two line plunges by Slansky had put the ball on Stratford's 35. Sullivan barked out Clint's name. Clint grabbed his helmet, which had been resting between his feet, and raced to the coach's side.

"Tell them to try 87," Sullivan said. When the referee's whistle stopped the next play, he slapped Clint in the seat of the pants. "Get in there!"

Eighty-seven was a touchdown play and worked best

when the defense had tightened and was ganging up on running plays. Walt would fade back to pass, fake a pass, and then pitch-out to Clint, who would run wide around left end. Clint would decoy the tacklers and then lateral to Ralph, who would be trailing him.

When Clint gave Walt the coach's instructions, Walt nodded grimly. "Let's go!"

It worked like a charm. Clint lateraled smoothly to Ralph just before he crossed the line of scrimmage. Then he slammed into two black jerseys who had been bearing down on him. Ralph's speed and shiftiness did the rest. He went down the sideline with breathless speed. He was tripped up on the 5, and one knee almost touched the ground, but he recovered and loped into the end zone. The roar of the crowd rolled over the field in waves. With a cocky gesture, Ralph turned and waved at the Monroe stands. The answering cheer he got was good-natured.

On the try-for-point, Paul did his usual superb job of kicking, and Monroe led by a score of 14–6.

After that, things got very tough. The Stratford Bulldogs seemed to be counter-punchers. It took the sting of a Monroe touchdown to make them give their best. They battered and fought their way to the Cougar 30. They shifted into the single wing, and the old Statue of Liberty play shaped up. The tailback took the pass directly from center and drew back his arm. The wing-back circled behind him and pretended to take the ball. He did a good job of faking as he ran wide.

Suddenly the tailback heaved a long one directly down the middle to the right end. Ralph and Clint went into the air with him, but the end had the reach on them. The ball danced on the tips of his fingers for a moment, and then he had it, and then he went down.

The ball rested on the 5. The Bulldog fullback charged into the middle of the line and went over the goal line headfirst. As the teams lined up again, the Stratford fans pleaded mightily for that extra point. But the hard-charging Cougars again hurried the kicker, and again he missed. The score was Monroe, 14; Stratford, 12.

They came into the closing minutes of the fourth quarter with the score the same. Monroe had the ball on their own 40. On a quarterback sneak, Walt was hit head on by a linebacker. Walt flew one way, and the ball flew the other. There was a wild scramble for the crazily bouncing ball, and an ensuing pile-up. When the pile was untangled, a grinning player in a black jersey cuddled the ball.

Walt went back to his safety position, muttering darkly.

Playing desperate ball, fighting against time, the Stratford Bulldogs hammered and pounded their way to the 10-yard line. There were only seconds left to play, probably not more than time for one play left. A skinny kid dashed onto the field from the Stratford bench, and the umpire blew his horn for a substitution.

A moment later, the Bulldogs went into place-kick formation.

Now the red-jerseyed Cougars rallied their defenses, yelling at each other, nodding grimly in reply. They had to block that kick. Clint reminded himself that it would be a dead ball if the kick was blocked. A great silence hung over the stands.

The ball spiraled back to the holder. This time the Stratford line would not yield. The kicker swung his leg, his toe plunked into the ball. The gun sounded, ending the game. Every eye in the stadium was on the ball. And the ball arced end-over-end, straight and true between the uprights. It was a field goal and three points. The game ended with the score Monroe, 14; Stratford, 15.

The black jerseys carried their kicker off the field on their shoulders. The Stratford fans were laughing, calling to one another, slapping backs. The Monroe rooters were quiet and subdued, and kept looking at the scoreboard as if to confirm what they had seen.

Walt trudged off the field, head down, the very picture of dejection. His fumble had set up the Bulldog goal. Clint went over and put his arm around Walt's shoulders and walked with him. "It was just one of those things, Walt. I did the same thing. Just a bad break—"

"Yeah . . . I know. Thanks, Clint," Walt said glumly.

The sun was below the rim of the stadium. The sky was a pale green. Clint saw Judy standing on the sideline. She wore her red sweater with the white *M* on front. Her face was sober. Clint stopped beside her.

"Don't look so sad, honey. We can't win them all, I guess."

"But it was so close," she said. "It's been a bad day all around. Will I see you tonight, Clint?"

"Sure thing. What's the trouble? Anything we can't handle?"

"Maybe," she said slowly. "I'll tell you tonight. You played a good game, Clint. I'm proud of you."

He wanted to tell her that she made him proud too. That whenever he thought "She's my girl," it made his heart swell inside him. When they were together, he was always more than when he was alone. He wanted to tell her these things, but he couldn't find the words.

"See you tonight," he said softly.

CHAPTER SEVEN

CLINT AND HIS FATHER talked over the ball game at the dinner table. Clint was calm. A lost game wasn't exactly a shot in the arm, but they had given their best. So a fellow could keep his head up and look at people with no shame. As far as Clint was concerned, the game was in the past. Things were moving too swiftly these days to waste himself in regret.

"It certainly doesn't put you out of the running for the championship," his father said. "Anything can happen in football."

"That's right," Clint agreed.

Only half of Clint's mind was on what they were saying. He was wondering what Judy wanted to see him about, and what had caused her worried look.

After dinner he helped his mother with the dishes and left the house. It was heavy dusk as he drove toward Judy's in his own car. His body ached from the exertions of the afternoon.

Mr. Harlin and Debby were raking leaves in the front yard, stirring up a dry, dusty odor. They greeted him cheerfully.

Clint spoke to them and went on to the house. He found Judy alone in the living room. Judy was moderately cheerful. "The way you looked this afternoon, I thought something terrible must have happened," Clint said. "Or was that just because we lost the game?"

"Losing the game was part of it," she admitted. "But there's something else."

"Well, what—?"

She jumped up. "I can show you better than tell you. Just a moment and I'll get my coat."

She went into the bedroom and reappeared wearing a blue coat of soft wool. They left the house and walked down the sidewalk. After half a block, they turned to the right. She stopped him before a modest white frame house. Taking a flashlight from the pocket of her coat, she played the beam over the front of the house. The windows were shattered. The rooms beyond the broken panes looked empty and ghostly in the pale beam of light.

"Every window in the house—broken," Judy said.

He frowned. "This is the house the Washingtons intended to buy, isn't it?"

"They *have* bought it."

"I didn't know that. When did it happen?"

"Only yesterday. They meant to start moving in tomorrow. Then this happened."

"Maybe it was just some kids up to their ornery pranks."

Her tone was sharp. "It *was* just some kids. But they did it because of what they had heard their parents say, and because they were sure they wouldn't be punished. Debby heard one of the youngsters bragging about the incident. He was saying that this is just a warning as to what will happen if the Washingtons move in."

"Do the Washingtons know about the windows?"

"Sure. They came over here early this morning. Leona came to tell me what had happened. She was biting her lip all the time to keep from crying. They were so proud of the house."

Bitterness surged up in Clint. He remembered how unhappy Jeff had looked before the game, and understood. He remembered how Jeff had played the game with a kind of angry desperation.

"Are the Washingtons going to move in, in spite of this?" he asked.

"No. They've decided to wait. But they were awfully confused this morning. Mr. Washington said that it would be almost impossible for them to stay where they are and pay rent and make house payments at the same time."

Clint turned and looked across the street. The new houses of the Vanderpool project loomed darkly in the evening light. He had seen them in the daytime. They were all nice houses, built in the modern manner with big windows and wide eaves.

"What can we do?" he asked Judy.

"I think there are things that can be done. But we can't do anything tonight—except maybe go and see Jeff and Leona and try to cheer them up a little."

"That's an idea. Let's go."

While they were riding across town, Judy said, "I think we ought to go and visit the people in my neighborhood and talk about the Washingtons. At least we can find out which ones are against them."

"Just you and me?"

"Yes—along with the minister of my church. I'm sure that I can count on him. I thought about it, and I decided that if we got a large group to call on those people they'd think we were trying to pressure them, and we'd get just that much more resistance."

"It's not going to be easy," Clint declared.

"Of course it isn't. Hardly anything is easy. But we've got to make a start somewhere." She paused and added, "I think there's something you fellows on the football team could do. The boys who broke those windows were just youngsters. You know how most boys of that age hero-worship football players. If it was made clear to them that some of Monroe's best players were on the Washingtons' side, it would make an impression on their slightly used little minds."

"We can't just give them a big-brotherly talk. Kids aren't much impressed by talk."

"Yes, but suppose that you replaced those broken windows some afternoon? The small fry would come around to see what was going on. They'd get the idea." She added, "Who'd help us?"

"Well, Paul, first of all. Then Archie, and Harry Diamond, and a few others."

Clint pulled up in front of the Washington place. He saw Jeff over in the vacant lot, tending a leaf fire. They got out of the car, and Judy went toward the house while Clint cut across the yard to see Jeff. The leaf smoke was a tangy fragrance in the evening air.

Jeff's teeth made a white flash as he smiled. "Hello, Clint. How're you doin'?"

"Okay, Jeff. Considering that we got whupped this afternoon, I feel pretty good."

The flames that licked at the dry leaves were bright orange in the dark. The light danced on Jeff's face. He said, "The first two games began to give me the idea that football wasn't such a tough game, after all. But I learned today. It was a rugged game. And it's no fun to get beat."

"It's no fun to get beat," Clint agreed. He picked up some leaves, tossed them on the fire. "Judy and I went over to see your house this evening. I'm sorry about what happened."

Jeff's face was sober. He said nothing.

"Judy and I are going to try and straighten things out so that you can move in without trouble," Clint said.

Jeff laughed, but there was no humor in it. "Just like that, you're going to do it, eh? All of a sudden those people are going to quit hating us and put out the welcome mat." His eyes were cool. "How're you going to do this miracle?"

Clint suddenly felt like a small boy faced with problems too big for him. It made him angry. "We're trying! You make it sound completely hopeless. If it's hopeless, why did you let your dad buy the place?"

Jeff's shoulders sagged over the rake handle. "I'm sorry, Clint. I was taking my spite out on you. But it looks as if we bit off more than we can chew. We wanted that place, so we went ahead and bought it without giving too much thought to what might happen. It's sure hard to give that place up. But I'm convinced that we never should have bought it. We're going to try and get our down payment money back, and if we can't, we'll let it go and charge it up to experience. Yes, sir! This time the Washingtons really goofed."

Clint kicked at the fire. "You're licked, huh?"

Jeff's voice raised a tone. "Not as a human being, I'm not. But I'm not much good at forcing myself into places where I'm not wanted. Let them keep their old neighborhood all to themselves. We'll get along all right. But don't you get the idea that I'm licked. I've just got some pride—that's all."

"You let one problem lick you and you're liable to let others lick you, too."

Jeff looked at him with a quizzical smile. "What's come over you lately, Clint? I've known you for a long time and it's been my idea that Clint Thomas was al-

[116]

ways for Clint Thomas. Now you're getting mixed up in the problems of the Washington family. What happened to you?"

"I changed, Jeff. Maybe other people can change, too. But you don't seem to think so."

"Well, I guess you've got a point there, Clint. I guess things have been getting me down. You get to believing that nothing will work out. You try maybe, but you expect to be disappointed. My dad works hard at a job he doesn't like. It seems that he should be able to spend the money that he earns in the way he wants. I feel kind of funny saying it, but this is a free country, isn't it? All we want is a decent house. Sometimes it looks as if they don't want us to have anything at all."

"I'm on your side, Jeff." And with the statement, Clint suddenly had a deep belief in his rightness.

"Well, you make me feel better, Clint. I'll tell you something. I was thinking about quittin' football after today's game. I like football. I like being part of the team, even if some of the fellows do treat me cool. But you've got to feel as if you belong a little bit to play a game like football. And when I saw what someone did to our house, I just didn't feel as if I belonged. It took the heart out of me."

"For a guy with no heart, you played quite a game today," Clint said dryly.

"I'll tell you something. I wasn't playing for *our* team. I was playing *against* the other team. I was mad clear through, and I was taking it out on those boys."

"It's too bad we all didn't get mad like that. We'd have won, then." Clint paused and added, "You're really quitting the team?"

"No, I guess not. Like I said, you've made me feel better. I'll stick it out for a while yet."

"Good boy," Clint said.

Judy and Leona came out of the house and joined them. They talked only about general things then, standing by the fire. When the flames died down, Jeff turned the leaves over with the rake and sparks flew up into the darkness. The fire burned brightly again. There was a new feeling of friendliness among them as they stood there. There was a warmth in Jeff's voice that had been reserved earlier only for Paul.

When they said good night, Clint added, "I hope you won't give up the house before Judy and I have had a try with our plan. If you can just wait a while—"

"I'll tell Dad," Jeff said. "I kind of hate to. I don't like to get his hopes up, and then see him disappointed again."

"Give us just a week," Judy suggested. "If we haven't made any progress by then, you can go ahead with your plans. A week isn't very long, Jeff."

"No, I guess it isn't. I'll get Dad to wait."

Clint and Judy stopped at the Malt Shop on their way home. There was the usual Saturday night crowd. Ralph was sitting in a front booth with several others. He and Clint exchanged glances. Ralph gave him a casual nod, but he did not smile and his dark eyes were cool.

They found Archie Strong and Harry Diamond at a table toward the rear of the room. "Sit down here, kids," Archie welcomed them. "Plenty of room."

They took chairs, and while they were waiting for the waitress, Judy told Archie and Harry about the broken windows and their plan for replacing them.

"You can count on me," Archie said, the moment she had finished.

"Me, too," Harry added. "But when will we do it? We practice football every evening, and play a game on Saturday."

"The coach will let us off one afternoon," Archie said.

"Why not Monday, then?" Clint suggested.

Archie nodded. "Sure. During the day we'll talk with fellas on the squad and see how many are with us. Then we'll ask Sully for the afternoon off."

Harry smiled grimly and jerked his head toward the front of the room. "There's a guy that we can talk to right now."

"Ralph? You'd be wasting your breath," Archie said. "That boy has a closed mind."

"Yeah. I was only kiddin'. But he's a good example of the kind of guys that are against us. It's not going to be easy to talk to some of them."

"Nothing is easy," Clint said.

The waitress came and thumped two milk shakes on the table before Archie and Harry. Archie lifted his glass, grinned, and said, "You're wrong, Clint. This is easy." And he drained a third of the glass in a gulp.

The rest of the evening, Clint had never been more alive. They were in a fight, and they had found comrades. And Clint had the feeling that what they were doing was very important.

By practice time on Monday, they had ten fellows lined up with them. Clint had been surprised at how favorably their idea had been received. Among those who refused, some had said no only because they did not want to miss practice. Others were just indifferent. Those who were actually hostile were in the minority.

Sullivan must have got wind of what was going on, for he showed no surprise when Clint and Archie walked into his office. He smiled at them and looked through the doorway at the others waiting outside.

"Don't tell me that you guys are going on a strike," he said jokingly. "What do you want? Less harsh words, shorter practice hours, vanilla flavoring in the water bucket?"

Clint laughed. "Naw. We came to ask—"

The coach interrupted him with a wave of his hand. "I know. And you're free to go. But I'll work you twice as hard tomorrow night."

"Okay, Coach."

They climbed the stairs that led out of the dressing room in a group. They passed several players coming down who looked at them sorrowfully, as though they felt they were being left out of something. "It's your own fault," Clint muttered. "We invited you."

Clint, Paul, Jeff, and three others rode downtown in Clint's car to pick up materials. The rest of the group went directly to the house, riding in Harry Diamond's car.

Clint and Jeff went into the paint and glass store and got the putty, points, and putty knives that Mr. Washington had ordered and paid for. The window glass had been delivered to the house.

Everyone was in a good mood when they arrived at 920 Maple, the address of the Washingtons' house. Clint was proud to be part of the gang. In being here, every man made it clear that he thought the Washington family deserved a break. The gesture was not lost on Jeff. He was hustling around, hope in his eyes.

Billy Berg, substitute quarterback, was chinning himself on a low branch of a tree in the front yard. Walt Tracy and another fellow were in the middle of the street sparring. "If this gang doesn't attract attention, the neighborhood is dead," Clint thought.

The gang went to work. They removed the broken pieces of glass from the windows, put in new glass, drove in the points, and sealed them with putty. Harry Diamond, who had experience in this kind of work, moved around and gave instructions and tidied up the putty with his own putty knife. It was slow work, but with ten of them on the job, they made good progress.

It wasn't long before housewives began peeking out of windows. They came out of their houses and congregated in small groups to chat curiously. A bunch of grammar school boys wandered up and stayed to stare. One redheaded, freckle-faced youngster approached Clint and Archie at a front window. "Whaddya doin'?"

Archie turned and eyed the boy. "Now, that's a stupid question if I ever heard one. What do you think we're doing?"

"Well, I guess you're putting in windows. But maybe you're just wasting your time. Maybe somebody will break them out again."

"Then we'll put them in again," Archie said. "But if someone messes up my work, and I find out who it is, I'll give him an awful walloping."

The boy gave him a leering, insolent look. "Gee, you talk awful, Mister. Who are you, anyway? You sure must be tough."

Archie looked at Clint with a pained expression on his broad face. "Where do these brats get all the sneering words? This one isn't dry behind the ears yet, and he talks like a private eye or something. Where do they pick it up?"

Clint shrugged. "The movies, and TV, I suppose."

Archie spoke to the boy. "Well, sonny, I can lick you and your TV set and your old man, too. My name is Archie Strong, and I can do more than just talk tough."

"Are you Archie Strong the football player?"

"That's me."

The boy's attitude underwent a subtle change. A measure of respect came into his voice. "I see every game. You're the captain, ain't you?"

"Co-captain," Archie corrected him. The rest of the small boys had moved in close. Archie spoke to all of them. "The rest of these guys are football players, too. And the fellow who is going to live in this house is the best player on the team."

The redheaded boy turned defiant again. "That's different! He's a nigger. And we don't want niggers in this neighborhood."

Archie reached out a big hand, grabbed the boy by the front of his shirt, and lifted him two feet off the ground. He stared into the frightened boy's eyes for a long moment, and then put him down.

"No—it isn't different," Archie said softly. "He's a good guy. Do you think we'd be putting windows in his house, missing practice, if he wasn't a good guy?"

The boy was scared and wary, ready to dodge if Archie reached for him again. He made no answer.

"Look, sonny, as one redhead to another, let's be on the level about this. Let's give these people a break. How would you like it if somebody broke all the windows in your house just because you have red hair? *You're different!* I'll bet you're the only kid in the block who has red hair."

The boy found his tongue. "No I ain't! My two sisters have red hair. Anyway, there ain't nothin' wrong with red hair."

"And there's nothing wrong with having a dark skin either, sonny. Just you remember that. Now get outa here. I'm busy and you bother me."

The boy ambled away, the others following. They looked back at Archie with curious, puzzled glances.

"You've got to talk up to them," Archie told Clint, as he rolled putty between his hands. "The small fry are playing it tough these days. You've got to talk to them in a language they understand. You can't pat them on top of the head and tell them to be good boys. They'd laugh in your face."

"A little patting in the proper place with a hair brush would do a lot of good," Clint said.

Archie shrugged. "That's out of style. We're supposed to let the little darlings do anything they please. If we don't, they're liable to be inhabited when they grow up."

"You mean inhibited," Clint laughed. He added, "Well, a lot of high school kids are no better."

"Amen, brother," Archie agreed.

They finished the job in the chill shadows of late afternoon. The gang gathered on the front sidewalk and stood there a few minutes to admire their work. It was near sunset and the new front windows reflected the yellow glow of the sun's slanting rays. The house looked whole again.

Jeff said, "Looks fine—mighty fine. I'm sure appreciating what you guys have done."

"You just keep on playing ball like you did Saturday, and we'll call it square," Walt said. "Right, gang?"

There were words of agreement. Someone said, "If they break the windows out again, I'm going to feel like breaking some heads."

Clint still had to take Paul home. He dropped Jeff on the way. He drove home from Slansky's in near darkness, and his mother and father had finished eating when he came into the house. But they were still at the table, lingering over their coffee.

"Well, young man, what held you up?" his father asked sharply.

Clint took his chair at the table and explained the reason for his lateness, while his mother brought his plate of food from the kitchen. George Thomas' expression changed as he listened. Finally, he nodded approvingly.

"You boys did a good thing. It might have some real effect. Anyway, it will give the people in that neighborhood something to think about." His voice stopped and then started again. "What I'm wondering is whether this problem is going to remain localized in that neighborhood, or whether the whole town is going to take sides. Seems that everyone who comes into the store knows what's going on. Maybe it will be a good thing if the trouble spreads. We'll get this thing settled once and for all."

"What gets me is that the trouble is really over nothing at all," Clint declared. "No part of it makes sense. The Washingtons are good people. They'll keep the place nice, and they won't cause anybody any trouble. The things those people are afraid of won't happen."

George Thomas nodded gravely. "You're right. But groundless fears have caused a lot of misery in this old world."

CHAPTER EIGHT

CLINT MET JUDY at her locker after history class next morning. The long hall hummed with many voices. There was the sound of laughter, footsteps, the slam of locker doors. Judy's clear green eyes looked at him personally and approvingly.

"I went over and looked at the house this morning. The windows look fine."

Clint smiled. "Don't tell me that they're still intact."

"They were as of eight A.M." She closed the door of her locker. "Are you going to be busy tonight?"

He decided to tease her. "Yes. I've got a date."

"Who with?"

"Oh, a girl I met," he said lightly.

Her eyes searched his face to see if he was joking. He rubbed his hand across his mouth to hide a smile. But his expression gave him away. She gave him a small push. "I knew you were joking."

"No, you didn't," he said. "You were jealous. You do like me, don't you?"

She gave her head a toss. "I refuse to answer."

"On what grounds?"

"Any old grounds."

They laughed together and then sobered. She said, "If you're not busy tonight, I thought we could visit in my neighborhood and talk about the Washingtons. I told Dr. McCray about the situation on Sunday and he said that he'd be glad to make some calls with us."

Clint was suddenly annoyed. Putting in the windows had been all right, but he didn't like this part of the game. Talking with people, arguing with people, trying to make them see things your way—the thing had no appeal for him. And he didn't much care for the idea of going with a minister. He felt ill at ease with ministers. He had always thought they were kind of strange. He didn't know why. He just had the feeling that they were kind of funny.

Judy read his thoughts with deadly intuition. "I know that this part isn't going to be pleasant. But we can't quit because of that, can we? You don't give up in a football game just because the going gets rough, do you?"

"No. But this is different," he said irritably. "I don't like to go around bothering people."

Her temper flared, quickly, like the spurt of a lighted match. "Bothering them! They're the ones who are bothering people. Of course, if you don't want to go, I'll get someone else."

He gave her a straight look. She looked right back at

him, not dodging a thing. They were on the verge of a spat. He gave in. "You don't have to be so tough about it."

Her face softened. "You'll come, won't you?"

"Sure. I'll be there. Is seven o'clock all right?"

"That will be fine."

He could see that she was pleased. The buzzer sounded through the halls and she gave his arm a quick pat and was gone.

There was an undercurrent of tension within the squad on the practice field that afternoon. The group that had missed practice the previous evening had made their position clear. They were for Jeff. The group hostile to Jeff, led by Ralph, now felt that they had to show their attitude. As a result, a good number of players on the field weren't speaking. And yet, every player worked hard. Harder, perhaps, than if they had been one big happy family. It was a large squad, and every man knew that if he began to let down, someone else was eager to take his place.

Coach Sullivan and Tucker walked slowly from the field after the squad had been sent to the showers.

"It may not hurt the team a bit, if it doesn't go too far," Sullivan said. "I've had teams where the backfield hated the linemen, and the linemen hated the backfield, and the whole team hated me—well, a little bit, anyway. And I still had good, clean, fighting teams. Dissension within a squad doesn't mean that it's going to fly apart. I'd rather have a little dissension. It's more normal. And if you've got the talent, and the boys really want to play, you'll have a good team."

"The thing that worries me is that they're too serious," Tucker observed. "It's a rough game and they need to let off steam. I like to see some horseplay in the dressing room. But tonight, that room was mighty quiet before practice. If they keep their feelings bottled up, things are eventually going to blow."

Sullivan wagged his head. "The trouble is over the Washington boy. And yet it isn't his fault. There's one thing on which I won't back down. As long as Jeff wants to play, and as long as he plays as well as he does, he stays on the team."

"You're right," Tucker agreed. "If we got rid of that boy, we'd lose the respect of the whole squad. I believe that. I believe that even the boys who are against Jeff wouldn't want to see him denied the right to play. They might not admit it, but I think it's true."

Sullivan tugged at the bill of his baseball cap. "Why coaches grow gray! There must be easier ways to make a living."

That evening, after dark, Clint drove to Judy's. A car was there ahead of him, parked at the curb. Clint met its owner in the Harlin's living room. Mr. Harlin introduced the Reverend Dr. McCray. The minister was a surprise to Clint. He had expected an elderly, serious, aesthetic man. Instead, McCray was young, tall, and athletic-looking. He had a ready laugh and spoke in a booming voice.

His smiling, sharp eyes looked directly into Clint's. "I saw you play football last Saturday, Clint. Fine game."

"Well—thanks."

"Dr. McCray used to play football too," Mr. Harlin informed Clint.

"Oh? Where did you play?" Clint asked.

"At a small college in the Middle West," the minister replied. "We never made the headlines. But we played better ball than you might suppose. And we had a lot of fun."

Clint liked the man. The ordeal of calling on people might not be so bad after all.

Judy came from the kitchen where she had been helping her mother with the dishes, got her coat, and the three of them left the house. The night was clear and fine. There was a moon, and shafts of pale cold light came through the branches of the trees. Clint took Judy's hand in his and they walked with their shoulders touching. He could smell the sweetness of some perfume that she wore.

"Who's first?" Judy asked.

"That's easy," Dr. McCray said. "Mr. and Mrs. Pfost live only two doors away from the Washington house. They're members of my congregation."

"Then they should be on our side."

Dr. McCray laughed softly. "I'm not so sure. Mr. Pfost has always been something of a mystery to me. He's an austere man. But anyway, we'll see how they stand. And if they're friendly at all, maybe they can tell us how their neighbors feel. In a situation like this, there are usually one or two who are the leaders. The rest are followers. If we can find out who the ringleader is in this attempt to keep the Washingtons out, we can go directly to him, or her, and save ourselves a lot of trouble."

"Sounds reasonable to me," Clint said, as they turned in at the walk of the Pfost home.

Mr. Pfost answered the doorbell, pipe in mouth, and newspaper in hand. He was a middle-aged man with a shiny bald head. He smiled when he saw Dr. McCray. He took his pipe from his mouth and said, "Come in —come in."

Clint was introduced to Mr. and Mrs. Pfost. Judy had met them before. Clint saw the puzzled looks on the Pfosts' faces as they doubtless wondered why the minister had come calling with two young people in tow. Dr. McCray quickly eased their curiosity.

As soon as they were seated, he said, "I'll come right to the point, folks. This isn't merely a social call. We're here to talk about the Washingtons."

Mr. Pfost looked at him blankly. "The Washingtons?"

"The Negro family who bought the house."

"Oh," Mr. Pfost said. There was an awkward pause. "I didn't know that was their name."

Dr. McCray's voice was earnest. "We're concerned about this problem—Judy and Clint because they are friends of the Washington children, and I because—it's my duty to speak out for what I think is right. Now, I've talked with a number of people in the past few days who know the Washingtons, and I was told that they are an average, law-abiding, hard-working family. So, I can see no good reason why they should not be permitted to improve themselves, which we Americans proudly proclaim to the rest of the world is the privilege of citizens of our country."

Mr. and Mrs. Pfost seemed uncomfortable. Their expressions were serious. Mr. Pfost began to suck on the stem of his pipe, but the pipe had gone out and it made a rattling sound. He suddenly realized what he was doing and put the pipe into his pocket.

Dr. McCray looked at them carefully. "I believe that you're not in favor of having the Washingtons for neighbors. Isn't that right?"

Mr. Pfost side-stepped the doctor's question. "There's a lot of talk about what will happen to the neighborhood if we let those people move in. They say that our property value will go down, and we'll be encouraging more of them to move in, and it will make this an undesirable neighborhood. Now, me and Grace believe in brotherly love just as much as anybody. But we worked hard to buy this place and we don't want to see our work undone. We don't have any race prejudice at all. We just figure that if they'll leave us alone, we'll leave them alone."

Dr. McCray nodded his head, not in agreement, but as though he had heard what he expected to hear. "By leaving them alone, I suppose you mean that they should stay where they are."

"Mmmmm—yes. I guess you could say that."

Dr. McCray ran a big fist along his jaw. "If the Washingtons were just accepted, there would be no reason why the value of your property should be lowered."

Mr. Pfost's voice grew stronger as he warmed to the discussion. "But they won't be accepted! Even if we accepted them, there are others who wouldn't. The effect would be just the same."

"In matters like this, our own opinions count for more than you think, Mr. Pfost. We can always fall back on the excuse that it does no good for us to take a positive stand on an issue because it might not do any good. If we all felt that way, nothing would be accomplished. It's only an excuse."

"You know what shacks most of the Negroes live in," Mrs. Pfost said timidly. She was a plain, tired-looking woman, and she spoke barely above a whisper. "Maybe they would let the place become an eyesore. With all those new homes across the street, this is one of the nicest sections in town. It would be a pity if we got undesirable people in here."

"The Washingtons would keep the place up nice," Clint put in. "The place where they live now is kept neat and clean."

"What gets me," Judy said, "is that if a white family wanted to buy, and even if they were ignorant and dirty, there probably wouldn't be any objection. People would simply make the best of it. There are plenty of white families you wouldn't want for neighbors. It seems to me that the Washingtons are being kept out just because they are Negroes. I don't think that's fair."

Mr. Pfost had his eyes fixed on a spot on the ceiling. "Maybe you folks are right, and again, maybe you're not. When it comes to the value of our property, we don't like to take chances."

"Mr. Pfost," Dr. McCray said, and his voice had taken on a quality that made all of them look at him, "I'm getting a little tired of hearing about the value of your property. I guess you know that I was a chaplain with our troops in Korea during the war. I saw boys there, both white and Negro, some of them scarcely older than Clint here, give their lives for the security of this country. And for your security too, Mr. Pfost. Your pleasant little home here was bought with more than just your own money and labor. I don't think you should forget that. You talk about the value of your property as though it were something sacred. What about the value of the lives of those boys, which were given so that all of us could stay free? Don't they impress you?"

The Pfosts had tensed to the doctor's words and now sat straight and stiff as pokers. They seemed at a loss for words.

"Now, you're being asked to take a risk—a very small risk—so that the Washingtons might have a chance for a better life. And it looks as if you don't want to take that chance. I'm afraid that my sermons of the past few years haven't reached you."

There was another silence. The stiff expressions on the faces of the Pfosts did not change. Dr. McCray did not spoil things—in Clint's opinion—by trying to smooth things over. He reached for his hat, got to his feet, and said, "Judy, Clint, and I have some more calls to make, so we'll be going. I hope you'll think things over, and maybe change your minds."

"It ain't likely," Mr. Pfost said coldly.

There were restrained "good nights" and they left the house.

Out on the sidewalk, Clint said respectfully, "You sure talked up to them."

"I try to be patient with people, Clint. It's the best policy. But I've worked with people so long that I can almost sense when I'm wasting my words. Talking will not change the ideas of people like the Pfosts. You've got to reach them in some other way. I wish I knew the way."

"Where do we go now?"

"The Jenkinses live in this next house," Judy said.

"I know them, and they've always seemed like nice folks to me."

Through a large, lighted window, Clint saw a man and woman and two youngsters seated before a television set. Next door, the Washington house was dark. They turned in at the walk. Judy knocked on the door, and when it was opened, briefly explained the reason for their call. Mr. Jenkins invited them in. The sound on the TV was softened so that the children could follow the program by sitting up close.

The Jenkinses were young people. Mr. Jenkins was smiling and cheerful. Clint noticed on a table a picture of him in naval officer's uniform.

"Concerning the Washingtons, I'm for letting them move in," he said. "In fact, I'll welcome them. I say let them move in, and if it turns out they're not nice people, then we've got a right to complain. But it seems to me, we haven't got any right to condemn them before we even know them. Isn't that right?"

"Mr. Jenkins, I think you're showing rare common sense," Dr. McCray said. "If everyone around here shared your attitude, there would be no trouble at all. Unfortunately, that's not the case."

"I guess that my time in the Navy has had a lot to do with my opinion," Mr. Jenkins said. "I saw a lot of the world and I found out that the big majority of people are colored. And I learned that when they're given the opportunity, those colored people are just as capable as us whites. And you can't look down your nose at the cultures of other countries just because they're different from our own. I—well, I guess I just changed my ideas."

Dr. McCray nodded understandingly. "I had much the same kind of experience. Maybe someday, when travel between the nations becomes common, we'll all come to know one another better."

"I'm afraid that we're about the only ones who are for the Washingtons," Mrs. Jenkins said. "A number are undecided, and a larger number are definitely hostile."

"Who would you say is the leader of the opposition?" Dr. McCray asked.

Mr. Jenkins shrugged. "The leader? That's easy. He doesn't live in this neighborhood, though. Mr. Vanderpool is the head man. He built those new homes across the street. Mr. Vanderpool has talked with every family on this street. He's pretty smooth, that Vanderpool. Almost makes you believe what he says in spite of yourself."

"I don't know the man," Dr. McCray said.

"His main argument is that if we let the Washingtons in we'll be letting down the bars for all kinds of undesirable people."

They chatted for a few more minutes with the Jenkinses and then left. They called at three more houses, but didn't get very far with the people they met. Suspicious and close-mouthed, they behaved as if they thought Dr. McCray was trying to put something over on them. After they left the third house, the doctor looked at his watch in the moonlight.

"I guess that's enough for this evening, isn't it? We can't do the whole job in one night."

Clint gave a short laugh. "Except for the Jenkinses, we didn't get anywhere at all."

"Now, I wouldn't say that, Clint. Maybe we gave them something to think about. Youth! You expect results so quickly. Now if I could just talk with Mr. Vanderpool and swing him over to our side . . ."

"Might as well try to move the Rock of Gibraltar," Clint said. "I've known the Vanderpools for a long time. Mr. Vanderpool isn't the kind who can be persuaded."

"Not ever?"

"Not that I've ever known, when he has a definite opinion on a subject. But if you want to have a try, I'll give you his address."

They reached Judy's home and stood and talked for a few minutes. "In football, we didn't let our opponents scare us because they were tough. We got in there and mixed it up with them. And sometimes we found that they weren't as tough as they looked." The minister grinned at Clint. "Isn't that the way it is?"

"I guess you're right," Clint agreed. "It's just that I'm not used to trying to talk people into things."

"It's the same principle, Clint. Talking is the harder way, that's all."

Dr. McCray bade them good night and went to his car and drove away. Clint watched the red glow of the taillights move down the street. "That man isn't afraid of anybody. I like him."

"Most people do," Judy said. "He speaks his mind and hurts feelings now and then. But they usually get over it."

Clint looked at her. Her face was lovely in the soft moonlight. A strand of hair had fallen across her forehead. He raised his hand and brushed it back in place.

"I think you're swell," he said softly.

"And I think you're wonderful."

He laughed. "Mutual admiration society, huh?"

"Definitely." She left him and walked toward the house. He stood there in the moonlight and watched until a light went on in the house.

It was the time of day when Clint was ready for a few minutes of relaxation. Wednesday was always a scrimmage day, and for nearly two hours the squad had been working hard. With a game against Kimball on Saturday, Sullivan had been polishing up their pass defense. Although Kimball had lost two and won only one, they were reputed to have an excellent aerial attack.

Halfway through practice, Clint had been mildly surprised to see Dr. McCray standing among a group of spectators on the sideline. There were always a number of watchers at practice. Some were fathers of boys on the squad, some were younger boys who dreamed of being players someday. And then there were the sports writers and photographers from Monroe's two daily papers.

When Sullivan blew his whistle and said, "That's all for today—everybody in!" Clint heaved a sigh of relief, jerked off his helmet, and walked over to have a word with the minister before he went to the dressing room.

Dr. McCray had a smile for him. "This is the first time I've been out to watch practice, Clint. I've enjoyed it. Brings back memories of my own football days."

"I imagine it would," Clint said.

Dr. McCray took Clint by the arm and led him out of earshot of the others, who were still standing around talking.

"I talked with Mr. Vanderpool this afternoon," the minister said, smiling and shaking his head, "and I must admit that your impression of the man must be right. He's sure a hard one to convince. In fact, I didn't get anywhere with him at all. I finally decided that if I'm ever going to make any headway with Mr. Vanderpool, it will have to be through his son. So I came out here today, hoping you can arrange a meeting between Ralph and me. I've never met the boy. I didn't even know which one he was on the field. Can you get us together?"

Clint scuffed a cleated shoe on the sod and frowned. "Yes, I suppose so. We're not on friendly terms any more, but I guess I don't mind asking him. When do you want to talk with him?"

"Well, right after you've showered and dressed—if that's all right with you."

"Okay, I'll ask him. But he'll probably guess what you want to talk to him about, and don't be surprised if he refuses to see you. Ralph's a chip off the old block when it comes to being stubborn."

The minister nodded. "Ask him nicely, Clint, and he'll probably come."

Clean and fresh from the shower, Clint was buttoning his shirt when he found Ralph quiet for a moment. It took an effort, but he walked over and said, "Ralph, there's a man upstairs who'd like to meet you."

Ralph was gazing into a mirror that was fastened to the door of his locker. He had put the mirror there himself. The other lockers did not have mirrors. Ralph was carefully knotting his tie, and he stood without speaking just long enough to make Clint feel a little foolish. Then he looked around with a slow smile on his lips.

"Don't tell me the college talent scouts are here already. I've been expecting them, but not so soon."

Clint managed a grin. "No. It's Dr. McCray. He's a minister."

Ralph's eyebrows shot up. "A minister! What in heaven's name does he want with me?" Then he laughed. "Say, that was a funny remark."

"Yeah," Clint said, without enthusiasm. "Do you want to see him?"

"I don't know. What does he want with me?"

"Why don't you ask *him?*"

Ralph's expression was suspicious. "Did you get him to come and talk to me about something?"

"Not on your life! It's his idea, and only his."

"All right, take me to him," Ralph said, with a shrug.

As Clint went back to his locker for his jacket, he thought that it was only curiosity that made Ralph consent. He told Paul what was up and asked him to wait in the car.

Clint and Ralph found Dr. McCray on the lawn outside the gymnasium. The minister was standing with his back to them, tall and erect in his tailored, dark suit. When Clint spoke his name, he swung around and his face broke into a smile.

Ralph acknowledged the introduction nicely, even charmingly. But as the doctor, wasting no time, began to talk about the Washingtons, the pleasantness went out of Ralph's face.

Dr. McCray's voice was kind and earnest. "You know Jeff from playing football with him, Ralph. Everyone I know says that Jeff is a nice fellow. You've probably discovered that for yourself. Now, I'm not suggesting that you have a heart-to-heart talk with your father. But young people often have a real influence on their parents, and if your heart tells you that the Washingtons deserve a break, then it would certainly do no harm if you told your father of your feelings—"

"And suppose that my feelings are the same as my father's," Ralph said, bristling. "Then what?"

Dr. McCray's face was sober. "I had hoped that, in

this one matter, you would disagree with your father."

"My father is an intelligent man. Why should I try to change his mind on a subject? He's had a lot more experience than I have. Why should I tell him what to do?"

"Because you belong to a different generation. And, in some matters, the young are wiser than the old. If that were not true, there would be no progress."

"Well, I'm not going to say anything to my father," Ralph declared. "We see eye to eye in this matter. I guess you mean well, but I think you're wrong. Anyway, why don't you mind your own business?"

"Young man," Dr. McCray said levelly, "these things *are* my business."

A deep anger throbbed in Clint. He'd had just about enough of Ralph. He was going to say something, but Ralph turned his back on them and walked away. Clint glanced at the minister. His face wore a small, defeated smile.

"I guess this isn't one of my days," he said. "Thanks anyway for bringing him to see me. I've got to be going now. So long, Clint."

"So long, Doctor."

Clint waited until the minister was out of sight around the corner of the building. Then, with long purposeful strides, he headed for Ralph, who had stopped on the sidewalk to talk with Jim Davis. Clint came up from behind, put his hand on Ralph's shoulder and spun him around. Ralph tensed and his eyes went hard. They stared at each other.

Clint's voice was tight with anger. "I don't think I ever saw you rightly before. You're just plain doggoned ornery. You had no reason to be nasty with Doctor McCray. None at all! He's a nice guy."

"If you're looking for trouble, you've come to the right place," Ralph gritted, his hands fisted.

Clint stared at him with dislike. "You're not so tough."

"Yeah? Well, go ahead and start something. Go ahead and hit me. Go ahead!"

"All right," Clint said quietly. He swung a short punch that caught Ralph on the point of the jaw and knocked him flat.

Ralph was on his feet in a moment, but Paul and Jim moved in suddenly and held them apart. They struggled for a few moments, but it was no use. "Take it easy," Paul said in Clint's ear.

"Calm down!" said someone else. "You dopes want to get kicked off the team? You've already got two strikes on you."

Their shoulders slumped and their arms were released. But there was still rage in their faces.

"I'll tell you something," Ralph yelled. "You guys seem to be willing to wreck everything on account of that Washington. But I got friends too, and maybe we're the ones who'll make some trouble. Just you wait and see. We're going to keep those Washingtons out of that house, and we're going to get rid of that one on the football team." He looked at Jim Davis for confirmation. "Isn't that right, Jim?"

"Don't talk so much!" Jim said.

"Let's break it up," someone said. "Coach sees us here and there'll really be trouble."

The group separated and drifted away. Clint and Paul went to the car. The familiar job of driving eased Clint's feelings and he was soon normal again, except for a cool hardness inside him that made him not at all sorry that he had hit Ralph.

"I don't see how he thinks he can get Jeff off the team," Clint said. "Maybe he was bluffing."

Paul stared ahead. "They might have something up their sleeves. We'll have to keep our eyes open."

They rode in silence for a time. Then Clint said, "You know, for years my dad has been telling me that you have to stand up and fight for things in this life. I didn't exactly know what he was driving at, but I do now."

"It's a fight, all right," Paul agreed. "I've known it for a long time."

CHAPTER NINE

THE COUGAR SQUAD moved into the dressing room at Cougar Bowl in a troop, cleated shoes scraping on the concrete floor. The second-stringers were exhilarated. Monroe had led Kimball all the way, and every player on the Cougar squad had gotten into the game. Monroe had won by three touchdowns, and the reserves were enthusiastically playing the game over again in words. Bill Montgomery, reserve left half, was the hero of the moment. He had romped through the entire Kimball defense in the closing minutes of play to score a touchdown.

But there was a noticeable silence among the first-string players as they banged open locker doors and began to peel off damp, chalk-dusted jerseys. For something had happened that cast a shadow over the victory.

The trouble had started in the Monroe stands. A small but noisy group of young men had begun to make catcalls and boo Jeff. Even when Jeff intercepted a

Kimball pass and raced seventy-five yards to score, they had booed him.

On the field the boos made most of the Cougars angry, and they blocked and tackled with spiteful force. The score would have been even more lopsided if Sullivan had kept in the first string.

Clint sat before his locker, unlacing his shoes. He stole glances at his teammates. Their faces were sober, their voices subdued. An explosive situation was building up. Clint could feel the tension in the air. Another thing that had been wrong on the field was that several Cougar players had been dogging it. Ralph, Jim Davis, Glen Hart and Elmer Spang had been loafing, and everybody knew it. The coach had taken them out of the game.

Their behavior, and the performance of the rowdy element in the stands, tied in too neatly to be mere coincidence, Clint thought. Was this Ralph's plan to get rid of Jeff? It might backfire. If Clint knew Sullivan, the coach would have Ralph and his pals on the carpet before many minutes had passed.

Sure enough, Sullivan stepped into the room and told Vanderpool, Davis, Hart, and Spang that he wanted to see them outside as soon as they were dressed. The four did not seem disturbed at the summons. They looked at each other with secret smiles, as if they had been expecting it.

When they had dressed and gone outside, the remaining first-stringers gathered together and waited. Only

Jeff stayed aloof. He sat on a bench, his face reserved and melancholy. Paul went over and sat beside him.

Some of the reserves drifted out of the room. Those who remained were quiet. After a time, the four boys came back into the room followed by Sullivan. They were trying to act devil-may-care, but were making a poor job of it. Their set smiles had a sickly tinge. Sullivan's face was very grim.

"All right," the coach snapped. "Get whatever personal belongings you have out of those lockers. Never mind your uniforms. The managers will take care of those."

Ralph took a jacket from his locker and swung around, his mouth hard. "You won't get away with this, Sullivan. You think you're the big cheese. You'll find out that some other people have some say, too."

"Vanderpool, one more word out of you and I'm liable to forget my position. Now get out of here!"

The boys went.

Sullivan paced up and down the concrete floor for nearly a minute. They watched him with a kind of awe. A fiery man, he ordinarily kept an iron grip on his temper. It took a lot to get him worked up like this. But when he stopped and spoke, his voice was steady.

"I called those boys outside because I knew they were letting down out there on the field today. I thought maybe they were taking it easy because we were in the lead right from the start. But the thing behind their attitude soon came out. They gave me an ultimatum! Either I put Jeff off the team or they were going to quit. Well, I didn't give them a chance to quit. I fired them. And I'm here to say that if there is anyone in this room who is in sympathy with those four, say so right now and turn in your uniform. Right now!"

There was a shuffling of feet. No one spoke.

"Some boys of high-school age aren't quite men enough to handle the prestige and popularity that comes with being a representative of the school on the football field," Sullivan went on. "They get the idea that they are indispensable. No one is indispensable. We'll plug the holes and we'll keep on playing." His voice rose. "They were good players. Our team may be weakened. But we'll go on trying and playing the game. If I had given in to those boys, the idea of playing the game would have been a mockery. That's all I've got to say. I believe you fellows will back me up."

There were words of agreement and nodded heads. Clint took a deep breath and let it out. Things were out in the open at last. Maybe it was for the best.

Just then a voice sliced the silence. Every eye in the room turned on Jeff. He was on his feet, and his face wore a stricken look that Clint had never seen before. He tapped his chest with a long forefinger.

He spoke quietly, but his voice, his whole body, shook with emotion. "All this trouble is on account of me, isn't it?"

No one moved, no one spoke.

Jeff looked around at them with a confused anxiety in his eyes. "Why do they pick me out to ride? Am I dirty or lazy? Am I a criminal? What's the matter with me? It's just because I'm colored, isn't it?" He went on with a catch in his voice, "Once I heard a white lady say that she felt sorry for me because I couldn't help it that I was a Negro. Just like it was something to be ashamed of. Well, let me tell you something. I'm not ashamed of being a Negro and I never will be. I guess I should turn in my suit so that you can call those guys back and tell 'em they can play. But I'm not going to. I'm not quittin'. I'm tired of being pushed around."

After that, Jeff went over and stood with his head in a locker.

Sullivan walked over and said, "I'm glad you're not quitting, Jeff. But whether you quit or not, the others aren't coming back. Not while I'm coach. The majority of fellows are on your side, Jeff. You're one of the few Negro students in our school. You're so much in the minority that it looks as if only white boys are capable of cruelty and prejudice. But deep down, people are pretty much the same everywhere. There are people of your race who have the same faults as some of us. So don't go judging all of us by what a few may do. That's not fair, either."

Jeff made no answer. Nor did he take his head out of the locker. Sullivan turned and left the room.

The fellows began to drift outside, talking in low voices, upset and troubled by the unexpected happenings of the past half hour. Clint and Paul and Jeff stayed behind. Someone had neglected to turn off a shower completely. The measured drip was a mournful sound. Paul went over and put his hand on Jeff's shoulder.

"Come on and ride home with Clint and me."

Jeff slowly turned around. He kept his head lowered, and Clint thought that he had been crying. "Okay," he mumbled.

Clint went back and stopped the drip of the shower. Then they went outside. It was getting late and a powder-blue haze lay over the stadium. Across the western sky there were long lines of crimson clouds. The air was sharp and fragrant. A feeling of sadness stole over Clint.

They crossed the playing field, quiet now, and went past the stands to Clint's car.

"Want to ride out to Paul's with me?" Clint asked.

Jeff had regained his composure. "No, thanks. I'd better get home. Dad was in the stands this afternoon. He might be worried about me."

No more was said until Jeff got out at his place. "Thanks, fellas," he said briefly, and walked toward the house.

As they rode on, Clint said, "He may not be quitting, but he's sure unhappy."

"Jeff tries hard to keep his chin up. But the idea that a Negro hasn't really got a chance has a pretty good hold on him. When things are going smoothly, he be-

[152]

gins to lose the idea. But when something happens, like it did today, he slips back into the old groove."

"We can't blame him for feeling that way today," Clint declared. "Those guys sure put on a lousy exhibition. Well, we'll see how they like sitting in the stands on Saturdays."

"Things have busted wide open," Clint told his mother and father that evening. "No telling what will happen now. There will be trouble on account of those guys getting fired. I'm on the coach's side, but I don't know what kind of a team we're going to have with those guys gone."

Clint had talked on the phone a few minutes before with Archie. Archie told him that Norwalk had beaten Stratford. So unbeaten Norwalk was in first place in the conference, with Stratford and Monroe tied for second place with one loss each. Monroe still had a chance for the championship. But with four first-string players gone, Clint thought bitterly, Monroe's hopes were probably gone, too.

"I could kick Ralph in the pants," Clint said. "He was behind the whole thing. I'll bet he even hired those guys in the stands to make a disturbance. It was all Ralph's doing."

"Or his father's," George Thomas suggested.

Clint nodded. "Probably both of them."

"I suppose Vanderpool will be after Sullivan's job,"

George Thomas said. "But he's going to have a fight on his hands. I'll see that people get the true picture of what happened if I have to ring every doorbell in town."

They talked on, and then Mrs. Thomas steered the conversation into a different channel. "The day after tomorrow is your birthday, Clint. What kind of a cake do you want this year?"

"How about angel food?"

"It's your favorite, isn't it?"

"Yep. Always has been." Clint stared at a dream. "I'll be eighteen. Hardly seems possible. I can remember when I thought eighteen was pretty old."

"I remember when I turned eighteen," his father said. "I *really* felt grown up. I debated for a week whether or not to grow a mustache."

Clint threw back his head and laughed. "Did you really? I mean, did you grow one?"

"No, I decided to wait until I got out of high school. Then I gave up the idea."

Clint went to his room. He had a date with Judy, but not until eight-thirty. So he took his time changing his clothes. He flicked on the radio. The local sports announcer was rehashing the Monroe–Kimball game. Clint guessed that it was a vanity, but he liked hearing his own name on the air. The sportscaster mentioned the "ungentlemanly conduct" of certain fans in the Monroe stands, but if he knew what had happened to the Monroe team after the game, he was keeping mum on the subject. And wisely, Clint thought. If the news spread around now, before tempers had a chance to cool, there might be serious trouble.

Despite the turmoil of the day, Clint felt good. He thought it might have something to do with his birthday coming up. Eighteen was a man's age. And in a manly way, he would have to face problems as they came to him. Anyway, he felt unbeatable.

He arrived at Judy's house at eight twenty-five. The house was completely dark. "That's funny," he muttered. He got out of the car and stood on the sidewalk, debating what to do. The sky was clouded and the evening was warm and windy. There wasn't a sound except for the low whine of the wind in the trees. He was a little angry. If she had had to go somewhere, at least she could have called and told him.

He was about ready to turn and go back to the car when he heard his name called from the front door of the house. It was Judy's voice. He walked up the sidewalk.

"What's the matter?" he asked. "Blow a fuse?"

"Something like that," she replied, laughing. "Come on in. We'll have it fixed in a jiffy."

He stepped into the darkened living room. "Golly, haven't you even got any candles? It's pitch black—"

Suddenly the lights went on and the house blazed full of light. To Clint's amazement, the living room was crowded with boys and girls. They laughed and hooted and shouted with glee at the blank expression on his face. For several moments he did not understand. He gazed dumbly. Then someone gave a signal and they sang: "Happy birthday to you . . . Happy birthday to you . . . Happy birthday, dear Clin-ton . . . Happy birthday to you."

Clint stood there, grinning and feeling pleasantly embarrassed in the presence of so much good feeling.

For a time there was a tense gayety in the room, everybody laughing and talking at once. But soon they relaxed, and Clint began to enjoy himself. Someone turned on the record player. The rug was rolled back and several couples started to dance.

Archie, Walt Tracy, Harry Diamond and several other football players were there. They formed a group and began to talk about what happened after the game. It was in all their minds and it was bound to come out.

After a few minutes, Judy came over and told them firmly that they were not to talk about the football situation. "I got up this party so that we could have a good time," she said. "Let's forget what happened just for this evening, huh? I feel bad about things, too. I invited Jeff and Leona to the party, but Leona said that Jeff feels pretty low after what happened this afternoon. So I guess they don't feel like coming. Come on, we're going to play some games."

They were only kid games, but everyone joined into the spirit of the thing and they had fun. They laughed at everything and at nothing, just because they were young and felt good. Judy handed out red and yellow paper hats for them to wear.

The climax of the party came when Mrs. Harlin brought a huge frosted cake into the dining room. It twinkled with eighteen lighted candles. Everyone gathered around the big table while Clint dragged in a deep breath and blew out the candles. He managed to put out every one, although he was red in the face and wheezing when he got through.

They sat down around the table. The silver coffee-pot glistened as Mrs. Harlin poured cupfuls of the good-smelling liquid. The cake was angel food.

"The cake is your mother's contribution, Clint," Mrs. Harlin said.

Clint chuckled. "She's an old faker! She asked me at the dinner table what kind of cake I wanted for my birthday. I guess she knew I'd say angel food."

After they had eaten, Judy brought a box full of gifts from the bedroom. She placed them before Clint on the table. He was flustered again. "Aw, you didn't need to buy me presents," he protested.

"Come on, open them up," Archie boomed. "If you can't use them, give them to me."

He got socks, ties and handkerchiefs. And of course some of his buddies had slipped in comic gifts. Like the imitation false teeth that bore a tag saying: "In case you lose your own before football season is over." It was signed by Archie.

Finally it was late and time to go. Cars had been parked around the corner of the block. Judy and Clint walked down the street with the others. Laughter and talk sounded in the stormy night air. Then there were cheerful good nights, and soon the last car had moved down the street and they were left alone.

"It was a swell party," Clint said, as they walked hand-in-hand back toward the house.

"I like parties," Judy said dreamily. When they came to the house, she said, "Wait here a moment," and hurried up the walk. She went into the house and returned with a gift-wrapped box. "It's my present for you. You can open it when you get home."

"Well for gosh sakes," Clint drawled. "All this fine treatment! I'll be spoiled rotten."

There was a street light at the corner and it shone dimly on her face while she looked up at him. Her lips tilted in a smile. "Here's something else," she whispered. And she put her arms around his neck and kissed him. Then she leaned back jauntily and said, "That's for being such a swell guy."

Before he could say anything, she turned and ran toward the house. "Good night," she called, before she closed the front door.

" 'Night," he murmured, not loud enough for her to hear him.

He was gay as he rode home—he even felt kind of lightheaded. He whistled the melody of a tune they had played several times on the record player, tapping his fingers on the steering wheel to keep time.

His parents were in bed when he arrived home, so he let himself in with his own key and silently climbed the carpeted stairs to his room. There he switched on the light and sat on his bed and opened Judy's gift. He lifted a fine pair of pigskin gloves from the box. He pulled them on his hands slowly, enjoying their soft feel and the good smell of new leather. They fitted perfectly, and he thought that he could have been certain they would. Judy was careful about things like that. He sat there for a while, just thinking. Then he went to bed.

There was a mysterious excitement in the air at school on Monday. Of course, everyone knew by now that four first-string players had been fired from the football squad. And they knew the reason. Everywhere —in classrooms, in the halls, in the cafeteria—there was talk and speculation among the students. But none of the teachers mentioned the subject, and it almost looked as though they had been told not to. Clint expected an assembly to be called, but that didn't happen, either. Things seemed to be just sort of hanging fire.

During the day, he had seen all the fellows who had been fired from the team. They were sullen and defiant and they hung together. They had friends from whom they sopped up sympathy and advice.

Jeff had come to school, which was a surprise to some. His attitude gave Clint hope. There was no martyred droop of the head, or shuffling of the feet. Jeff walked the halls ramrod straight, his dark eyes flashing around him in a challenging way. He wasn't being aggressive, but he wasn't dodging anything either. Clint felt a growing respect and admiration for the boy.

"I half expected him to quit," Clint told Paul, as they walked together toward the practice field, "in spite of what he said Saturday."

Paul nodded. "I'll bet he's considered it. But I bet too he just can't face going back to the way things used to be. He's taken some steps up the last couple of months, and it's going to take a lot to make him step down again."

"Does that apply to the house, too? Are they going to keep it?"

"I'm sure that they are. Jeff said that they're not going to move in until things quiet down, but they're not giving it up."

"Good," Clint said. "I'm glad to hear it."

On the field, before practice started, Sullivan had a few words for them. He paced up and down before the group, using his hands and arms in gestures to give emphasis to what he said.

"Now, I suppose some of you are inclined to think that this team has been hopelessly crippled because we've lost some first-string players," he said. "I want you to get that out of your heads right now! I'll tell you something, and I'm not saying it just to lift your spirits. On a football squad, the difference in playing ability between a first-stringer and a reserve is often very slight. It's enough to make a coach feel like he's indulging in guesswork when he lets one player stay in a game while another rides the bench. Every year, all over the country, coaches put in substitutes who suddenly catch on fire and break the game wide open. They make us coaches wonder if they've been hiding their talents, or if we were just too dumb to see them. A number of years ago I saw a Rose Bowl game in which a fourth-string quarterback named Doyle Nave completed four passes in a row in the closing minutes of the game. The game was between USC and Duke. Duke led by a score of 3–0 until Nave went into the game. He threw the last pass with forty-five seconds left to play. He fired it into the end zone where USC end Al Krueger caught it. USC won over Duke by the slender margin of 7–3.

"Now, this team is strong in reserve strength. If we work hard, there's no reason at all why we can't go ahead and win games. One thing more: the players who were fired from this team were fired because they objected to playing ball with Jeff. I assume that if any of you have similar objections, you wouldn't be here. So from now on we're a unified team." Sullivan clapped his hands. "All right, let's get to work! Ends and backs over here!"

"Linemen come with me!" Tucker yelled, as he walked toward the blocking and tackling dummies.

Sullivan's words renewed hopes that had been chill. They worked like beavers at practice. Bill Montgomery took Ralph's place at left half. The promotion had a good effect on him. He played well.

Clint himself felt a new weight of responsibility. He knew that, with Ralph gone, he'd be called upon to carry the ball more often. But his old doubts and fears about being a ball-carrier had disappeared. He felt confident.

That evening Clint confessed to his father his surprise that the teachers at school weren't saying anything about the present crisis. "I expected an assembly with the principal making a speech. Or at least for some of the teachers to have discussions in the classrooms. But they were mum."

"Any trouble between students? Any fights or loud discussions?"

Clint slowly shook his head from side to side. "No. Just a kind of coolness. There may have been a few words exchanged, but I didn't hear them."

George Thomas stroked his chin with his fist. "There's reason for the teachers keeping quiet at this time, Clint. Sullivan was in the store at noon and we talked about it. You see, our side has the advantage at present. Jeff is still on the team, and those who are against him aren't. Sometimes discussions can do more harm than good. There are arguments, people get mad. The impression that the principal and the teachers are trying to make is that there isn't any need to get up in public and defend Sullivan's action. They are trying to show that no explanation is necessary. Because Ralph and his gang are in the wrong." Mr. Thomas leaned forward in his chair. "That's what we want, Clint. We want it to be accepted as natural and right that the Washingtons have equal privileges as citizens of this country."

"But suppose the ones who are against us get up a meeting? Don't we talk back?"

"Of course. But it's their move. It's possible that they'll accept the situation as it is."

"I can't imagine Mr. Vanderpool accepting things as they are," Clint declared.

"Oh, he's been doing some talking, all right. He's really worked up. He didn't come to see me because he knew it wouldn't do any good. But he's talked with every other businessman in town, and the members of the school board, and anybody else who will listen. He wants Sullivan fired."

"Is he making any headway?"

"He has supporters. The people on his payroll and some of the businessmen who get the bulk of their orders from the Vanderpool Company. But even some of them only listen politely and say nothing." Mr. Thomas' face broke into a smile. "This minister, Dr. McCray, is following Vanderpool right up and tearing down his argument. That preacher is really a talker. I like him."

Clint frowned. "Do you really think all this is just

going to blow over, Dad? Sounds too good to be true."

"We'll just have to wait and see. I'll bet the way our football team makes out is going to have a lot to do with this matter. The people are really behind the team this year. If you fellows start losing games, Sullivan is going to become unpopular and his cause along with it. But if you win, their enthusiasm is liable to sweep the opinions of Vanderpool's crowd right out of town."

Clint looked at his father uncertainly. "That sure puts things on a shaky basis, doesn't it? Whether we win or not has nothing to do with the right and wrong of the matter."

"Ah," his father said, "but we're dealing with human nature. And human nature is a strange thing."

CHAPTER TEN

THERE WAS PROBABLY more pre-game excitement in
the city of Monroe before the game with Milton
than at any other time in the season. The Monroe Cougars had a different team, and the question in everyone's mind was: What kind of a team? The newspapers
had been kicking the question around and the town
seethed with curiosity.

The team itself had fallen victim to some of the
doubts expressed by fans and sports writers. It was a
quiet, serious squad that rode the bus to Milton the
day of the game. Several times Coach Sullivan tried to
break the moody spell by telling funny stories. The
polite laughter which inevitably followed would fizzle
into silence.

It was another bright sunshiny day. It was a dry country and storms when they came were not likely to last
long. They rode past quiet farms where shaggy brown
fields lay pleasant and warm-looking in the sunlight.
Clint saw a hay derrick standing beside a stack of hay,

and the past summer returned in a rush of memory. He and Paul fell to talking about small humorous things that happened in the hayfields and on several occasions Paul roared with laughter.

Across the aisle two reserve players looked at Paul reproachfully. Paul turned serious as he stared back at the boys. "Well, what the heck!" he yelled. "Are we going to a ball game, or a funeral? If you guys don't relax, it's liable to be a funeral, all right. You can't play ball when you're as tight as fiddle strings."

Someone laughed, probably because Paul usually didn't spout off that way, and then there were other laughs, and after that the tension eased noticeably.

During the pre-game warm-up, Clint squinted into the sun as his eyes swept the Monroe stands. He saw a bigger crowd than any that had traveled to see an away-from-home game. He wondered if Ralph and Jim Davis were up there. Clint supposed they would be rooting for the Milton Trojans today. If Monroe got beat, it would make Ralph Vanderpool and company look good.

The Trojans warming up at the other end of the field wore white jerseys with big red numerals. Their colors were really red and gold, but since the Cougars wore their red jerseys today, the Trojans had replaced their own red jerseys with white ones.

Then the squads retired to the sidelines, the captains conferred with the officials, the coin was tossed. With parting words of advice from their coaches, the starters took the field and lined up for the kickoff. Clint was a starter. Monroe was kicking off.

The game opened up in a kind of fury. Taking the kickoff, a fast, shifty Trojan back brought the crowd to its feet with a beautiful runback of thirty-five yards. On first and 10, the Trojan quarterback heaved a pass that clicked for twenty yards, and the ball rested on the Monroe 25. The fullback hit inside tackle for 7, and then off tackle for 8. And the ball was on the 10 and the Trojans were knocking on the door.

The Cougars yelled at each other in desperation as the Trojans huddled. "Stop 'em, gang—stop 'em! Let's go!"

But a quick pass to the left end in the end zone brought Milton's first score, and pandemonium to the Milton stands. The roar from the Milton stands kept up during the try-for-point, and rose to an even higher pitch when the ball struck an upright and bounced inside for the extra point.

Except for the cheerleaders and a few loyal student rooters, the Monroe stands were wrapped in quiet gloom. Clint could read their minds and almost hear the talk as he went to his position to wait for the Trojan kickoff.

"I guess the sports writers were right," he could imagine they were saying, "this team is shot."

Then Clint and the others heard voices from the stands. Voices which filled them with anger. The loud, raucous voices were aimed at Coach Sullivan.

"Bet you wish you had those players back now, Sullivan," they yelled tauntingly.

"We want Vanderpool!" someone else cried.

"You fired the men, Sullivan. Now all you've got left are boys!"

There was coarse, harsh laughter which a number of the fans picked up automatically. Some of the voices even began to cheer the Trojans. Clint looked around at his teammates. Did they feel as he did? Their faces were grim and square-jawed. They scuffed their cleats in the grass with impatient motions, waiting for the kickoff.

Paul took the spiraling ball. Slowly at first, and then with accelerating speed, he ran straight ahead. He used up his blockers in gaining twenty yards. Then two white jerseys came charging at him from opposite directions. He did not swerve in his course, but gambled on the chance of slicing between them. He leaned forward, work-hardened legs driving for all they were worth, knees lifting high. He made a poor target for a tackler. Runner and tacklers converged at the same moment, but the tacklers flew apart as though they had been hit by a bull. The impact tripped Paul up though, and he made a nose dive for the turf five yards farther on.

In the huddle, Walt spoke with an angry tremor in his voice. "Let's show 'em, gang. They can't talk to the coach like that. Let's make them eat their words. Spin 46 on 4. Let's go!"

Three brutal line smashes picked up ten yards. Then Walt called for Pass 57. It was a play they didn't use very often. Clint was the man-in-motion on the play, running wide to the left and then cutting downfield. Walt would fake a hand-off to Bill Montgomery, who would punch into the line. Jeff would go down and buttonhook back. Meanwhile, Walt would fade back and fire a long one to Clint. The deception of the play would be that the Trojans would be expecting Jeff to receive.

As Clint ran wide and then headed downfield, he had an odd sensation. He felt so sure that he would catch the ball, if it came anywhere near him, that in his mind's eye he could already see himself toting the ball for the goal line.

The pass was high. But he lengthened his stride and gauged the descent of the ball nicely. At the last moment, he leaped and plucked the leather easily out of the air. He hardly broke stride as he drew the ball to his body. Then he was racing down the sideline at top speed. He outran two white jerseys and side-stepped another, and moved into pay dirt standing up. The play had been good for fifty-five yards. The pass had traveled through the air for a good forty yards between Walt's hands and Clint's.

And now the Monroe stands came alive and burst into a roar of delight.

"Fickle, aren't they?" Paul drawled, as they lined up for the conversion attempt.

Paul tied the score with a clean boot between the uprights, the blue sky silhouetting the tumbling arc of the ball. It couldn't have been more perfect.

From that time on, the Cougars showed that as a team they were still of championship caliber. Confidence regained, they played with fire and speed and spirit. The Trojans, who had started out so brilliantly, bogged down and couldn't get started again. Before the half was over, the Cougars had added another touchdown to their score.

Bill Montgomery at left half, Ralph's old position, shook loose for several long runs during the second half. He was as hard to stop as a greased pig.

All of the Cougars played well, but it was really Clint's day. He played the finest game of his life. He was playing way over his head. Twice he intercepted Trojan passes, and on the second one he ran sixty yards through the whole Milton team for a touchdown. He did more than his share in making the final score read: Monroe, 33; Milton, 13.

In the hilarity of the dressing room afterward, Clint was quiet. He actually felt too good to be noisy. He didn't know which pleased him more—the fact that the team seemed strong as ever, or his own performance.

While they waited for the bus to pick them up outside the stadium, Coach Tucker came over and laid his hand on Clint's shoulder. "You really played ball out there today, boy."

Clint grinned and felt a warm glow inside.

"I've seen it happen a number of times," Tucker said. "A player keeps at a game and goes along for long periods at about the same level. Then, for some unknown reason, he steps up a level. I think that the sustained effort builds up a power that breaks through and makes him a better player than he ever was before. That happened to you, I think. Accept the fact and expect the same kind of performance from yourself in the future that you showed out there today." He paused and added, "I expect to hear your name mentioned in connection with some good college team in a few years, Clint."

Clint looked up at the rim of the stadium where red-and-gold pennants were rippling and snapping in the wind that came with sundown. His heart swelled. "Thanks, Tuck. I hope I can live up to your expectations."

Riding home, they got the results of the other games. Archie had a portable radio. He stuck the antenna out a window and the broadcasts came in loud and clear.

"And now for the results of high-school football games in the Big Seven Conference," a sportscaster was saying. "In an upset at Eaton this afternoon, the Eaton Huskies scored a victory over the strong Stratford Bulldogs. The score was 10–7. The Bulldogs rolled up far more yardage than their opponents, but seemed to lack the needed punch to get the ball over the goal line . . ."

In the bus, they looked around at each other in surprise and then drowned out the sportscaster's voice with cheers. Stratford beaten! That meant that they were in second place. They might even be tied for first—if Norwalk had been beaten.

"Pipe down!" Clint yelled. "Let's hear the rest."

Silence again descended on the bus. The sportscaster rattled off some scores, and then said: "At Norwalk this afternoon, the powerful Norwalk Mustangs tromped Oak Hill to the tune of 20–0. The big green team— green is the color of their uniforms and has nothing to do with their experience [chuckle]—carried the game to the Oak Hillers all the way. . . ."

There were groans and mutterings in the bus. Norwalk still led the conference. The sportscaster concluded his broadcast with a glowing account of the Monroe–Milton game.

"The Monroe Cougars took the field an unknown quantity because of the loss of several first-string players. But Coach Sullivan surprised everyone by fielding a team that looked as strong as ever. The Cougar line showed no weakness today, and the backfield was superb. Next Saturday is an open date on both the Norwalk and Monroe schedules. But should Norwalk be beaten two weeks from today, and if Monroe wins, the two teams will be tied for first place. Then the game between the Cougars and the Mustangs November 11 will be for the championship. Regardless of how the pattern shapes up, that should be a whale of a game. . . ."

After the radio was turned off, Clint rested his head on the back of the seat and gazed out the window. The light had begun to fade, and a bright star hung over the hills in the west. The tires on the pavement made a high-pitched monotonous sound. Phrases from the sportscast ran through his mind. "A whale of a game . . . a whale . . . a whale . . . a whale—"

Paul had to shake him awake when they arrived at the gym in Monroe. He had been fast asleep.

The days slipped by swiftly. Clint was so busy with studies and football that he and Judy never had time for more than a few words during the day. He saw her evenings sometimes, and when he couldn't go to her place he called her on the phone. They still talked a good deal about the Washingtons, less and less about Ralph Vanderpool and the unrest at school caused by the firing of the football players.

The trouble over the firing of the players had abated, until the new status of things was accepted by most everybody. Even the discharged players had seemingly accepted the fact that they were through for the season. Ralph had apparently lost some of his bitterness, and he said hello briefly to Clint when they met in the halls.

But the situation among the adults concerning the Washington family and the house had changed not at all, and in some ways was even worse. Jeff had told Clint that they had received a number of anonymous telephone calls advising them not to move into the house, the voices carrying veiled threats. Letters were sent regularly to the editors of the two newspapers concerning the issue. Both pro and con views were published.

The efforts of the anti-Washington crowd rose to new heights when they called a meeting for Saturday evening at Barnum Hall, a building that had once been a dance hall, but was now rented out for various meetings and gatherings.

A meeting to discuss the future welfare of our city, its homes and schools, the ads in the newspapers read. *The public is invited.*

However, word had gotten around that the meeting was really intended only for the anti-Washington people. The purpose of the meeting was to discuss ways of preventing the Washingtons, and any other "undesirable people," from moving into respectable, white neighborhoods.

But Clint learned that there would be at least one dissenter in the audience. He had talked with Dr. McCray one night on the practice field and the minister said that he was going to the meeting.

"There may be something that I can do," he said simply.

"Don't you want some moral support?" Clint asked. "How about some of us football players going with you?"

Dr. McCray thought about this and said, "Well, I think that would be all right if you pick a few steady fellows who can keep calm and will, under no conditions, create a disturbance. At a meeting like that, where emotions run high, the slightest thing can touch off a riot. Our side would gain nothing by that."

"What does that crowd want?"

"They won't be satisfied until the Washingtons give up the house. That's what they want, Clint."

When Clint took Paul home after practice Friday evening, Paul mentioned that he was going to cut wood the next day.

"We've got a fireplace, you know. That house is old, but the man who built the fireplace did a good job. It's as good as new. Big, too. You can put half a log in it."

"Need some help?" Clint asked. "I haven't a dog-goned thing to do tomorrow."

"Be glad to have you, if you really want to come."

"Think Jeff would like to come, too?"

"Probably. It wouldn't do any harm to drive past his place in the morning and ask him."

Clint picked Jeff up the next morning. They drove through the countryside where the ground was powdered with frost in the shady places. It was a prime fall morning, clear and cold. It made their blood stir.

Paul was glad to see them. They picked up a crosscut saw, an ax, a maul, and some wedges and went to the woods. They felled a giant tree on the Slansky property near the river and then bucked it into fireplace lengths with the saw. The sound of the crosscut saw vibrated keenly in the country silence. The odor of the river and the mud of the bottom lands mingled with the fragrance of sawdust and dry leaves.

At noon they took healthy appetites in to a dinner of chicken and dumplings that was fit for a gourmet. Jeff seemed to feel right at home in the Slansky household. His eyes were gay as he joined the friendly warmth around the table.

They went back to the woods after dinner, but were so gorged with food that they found it absolutely necessary to sit down and lean their backs against a log for a while before they could resume work. The sun was high and warm now. Clint gazed upward at the pattern the branches of tall trees made against the sky. A couple of melancholy crows were cawing lustily in one tree.

"Family squabble, I guess," Clint said, grinning.

"Sounds like my neighbors," Jeff drawled. "Man, those folks really raise a fuss sometimes."

By three o'clock they had hauled the last load of wood to the woodshed in Mr. Slansky's pickup truck. Before Clint and Jeff left for town, Mr. Slansky brought two big bags of choice Delicious apples for them to take home.

"I pick them out especial for my friends Cleent and Jeff," he said. "Eat plenty. Football players need much strength."

Driving down the lane, Clint almost ran over a chicken. "Darn things run right under your wheels," he grumbled.

The nearer they got to town, the less Jeff talked. "It did me good to get away for a while," he said, as they entered the city limits. "Sometimes I hate this town. I suppose you've heard about the meeting they're having tonight."

"Yeah," Clint said.

There was bitter irony in Jeff's voice. "The Washington family is really important in this town, isn't it? Important enough to have a lot of people get together just to talk about them. I suppose we should feel real good."

There was an uncomfortable silence. "I'm sorry, Jeff," Clint said then.

Jeff nodded slowly. "I know you are. I don't know how I'd keep going if it weren't for guys like you and Paul and Archie. You know this thing we call the ego? Well, it doesn't do a fellow's ego any good to have something happen like that meeting tonight. Makes him feel like a freak."

"I wouldn't worry about what people like that say, Jeff."

"I tell myself that all the time, but it doesn't seem to do much good."

Clint borrowed the family car that evening to go to the meeting. He wore his red letter-award sweater against the chill of the night. He drove about town picking up Archie, Walt, Harry Diamond, Bill Montgomery, and finally Dr. McCray. The doctor was jovial and entertaining as they rode across town toward Barnum Hall. But he sobered as they neared the hall and saw the number of cars that were parked at the curbs along the street.

"We've got more competition than I had counted on," he said.

The meeting was just getting under way when Dr. McCray led the file of boys to seats in a middle row. The group drew curious stares. The boys' red sweaters marked them as football players, and at the same time identified them as friends of Jeff Washington. They all sat on one bench, with Dr. McCray on the aisle.

The hall was nearly filled. Only a few benches at the back were empty. On a raised platform at the head of the room, a half-dozen men sat behind a long table. Clint recognized Mr. Vanderpool, and Mr. Pfost, the man he and Judy and the doctor had called on several weeks ago. A large United States flag hung on the wall behind the speaker's platform.

Clint looked around the room for Ralph, but did not see him. There were few young people in the hall.

Mr. Vanderpool introduced a Mr. Blakiston who made the first speech. He was a corpulent, baldheaded little man with a pompous air. His head shone under the unshaded light bulbs that hung from the ceiling. Mr. Blakiston went into a loud, long speech in which big-sounding words and rolling sentences counted for more than content. However, the gist of it all was that, in his opinion, segregation was an institution which had endured for a hundred years, and there was no good reason why it shouldn't endure for another hundred.

Mr. Blakiston sat down to a vigorous round of applause.

Next came Mr. Pfost. He was very nervous. He had evidently rehearsed, and he had notes to refer to. But in spite of that, he made a sorry thing of his speech. Most of the time he stared at a spot on the rear wall and stumbled slowly and haltingly through the complications of a problem that was clearly beyond him.

After Mr. Pfost, Mr. Vanderpool took the floor. Mr. Vanderpool had an important, composed air as he launched into his argument. It all boiled down to the idea that Mr. Vanderpool considered Negroes to be inferior, and he didn't want them moving into white neighborhoods. He shook his head angrily, tossing his white hair, as he spoke. This mannerism gave the idea that Mr. Vanderpool thought anyone was stupid who couldn't see things his way.

He closed his speech with the suggestion that the people sign a petition. The petition would state that the signers were against admitting Negroes into white neighborhoods. The petition would be shown to real estate brokers, with the threat of boycott if they did not comply. As for the Washingtons, maybe the number of signatures on the petition would convince them that it would be wise for them to give up their house.

Clint was enraged by the proceedings. Their arguments seemed cheap and meaningless. He looked sideways at Dr. McCray to see how he was taking all this. The minister seemed cool and collected.

Mr. Vanderpool signified that his speech was ended, and gestured toward pencils and paper on the table for those who wanted to sign. But before anybody could rise and make for the platform, Dr. McCray was on his feet.

"Mr. Chairman," he called out, "in the interest of fairness, will you permit me to address the audience?"

People twisted in their seats and stared at the minister, and Mr. Vanderpool considered him thoughtfully.

"We are fair-minded people," Mr. Vanderpool said. "Come ahead and have your say."

As the doctor walked up the aisle, the crowd began to murmur and titter and a few made catcalls. When he ascended the steps to the platform and stood before them, they quieted to give him a shrewd, appraising look. The tall straightness of the man, the composed attitude, evidently made an impression on the crowd, for they held their tongues and gave him their attention.

The contrast of hearing a professional speaker, after the clumsy efforts of those who had preceded him, was not lost on the crowd. The doctor spoke with power and conviction. He said exactly what he intended to say. Wisely, he did not berate his listeners with moral indignation for their stand. He used reason instead, stating the facts so clearly that Clint could scarcely see how any thinking person could deny his logic.

"Now, the main concern of one of the speakers here tonight was that he might lose money if the Washingtons became his neighbors," the doctor was saying. "He wasn't certain that he would lose money, but he thought there was that possibility. So he prefers to take no risk. My only answer to that is that I believe people are more precious than things—even the things that belong to Mr. Pfost. With the other speakers, the main objection to the Washingtons seemed to be based on the old theory that all Negroes are social and intellectual inferiors. Therefore, they are not to be granted the same privileges as whites. This idea, of course, goes back to pre-Civil War days. Well, we've changed a great many of our ideas since then, and it's about time we changed this one.

"In our time the scientists speak with authority and we listen. And what do they say about this theory that some races are inferior to others? They deny that any such inferiority exists! The anthropologists tell us that there are different levels of feeling and intelligence among individuals, but not among whole races. Why then, you may ask, is the great majority of scientists and inventors and thinkers found among the white peoples? It is because their abilities have been learned, and they have had access to learning. A Chinese boy might have a talent for mathematics, but if he is the son of a peasant and does not go to school he will never become a mathematician. There may be parents right in this hall who have a boy or girl with great latent musical ability.

But if that child has not the opportunity to play a musical instrument, he will never become a musician.

"So, when you point your fingers at Negroes in our country and say: 'These people do not deserve a chance because they are not our equals,' I say that you are confusing inferiority with lack of opportunity. My plea is not that you show sympathy toward a creature who is less intelligent or less capable than yourselves, but that you give opportunity to men and women who, through gross misunderstanding and prejudice, have not been able to show what they can do.

"Times are changing. In many of the larger cities all over the country the Negro is being given opportunities in industry and business and education that he would not have right here in our own town. We piously like to think that small-town people are more filled with brotherly love than the hurried people in large cities. We'd better wake up to the facts. About the only way we differ from our big-city cousins is that we are more resistant to change.

"It seems to me that our vision doesn't go very deep in this matter. We expect the Negro to pay taxes, to abide by the laws of the community, and to serve in the armed forces. We demand of him all the duties of citizenship. But we do not want to grant him the privileges of that citizenship. Is it kind, or fair, that we should expect a man to shoulder his share of the burdens, and then deny him his share of the privileges?"

Dr. McCray talked on, tearing down the other speakers' arguments point by point. In concluding, he said: "It is my hope that the Washington family will be permitted to move into the house that they bought. But even that, in my opinion, is not enough. Let's treat them like friends *after* they have moved in. Let's get rid of ignorance and prejudice and pride, and become acquainted with a new point of view. Let's not permit old ideas to hold us in an iron grip, as though we were trained animals, incapable of altering the results of early training.

"All of us are aware that the world is burdened with suffering. Each one of us can do his part in bringing some of it to an end. We can do this by not closing our hearts to the needs of others. Our great hope is for peace in the world. But peace will come only when we have defeated greed and selfishness and practice the ancient teaching: 'Therefore all things whatsoever ye would that men should do to you, do ye even so to them.' "

The minister nodded his head and said, "Thank you," and left the platform. Clint was elated. Unconsciously he applauded, and his friends joined in. But the rest of the hall was silent. Clint looked about him. Surely they would see the light after a talk like that. Certainly the doctor's words had awakened a response. But, for the most part, Clint saw blank closed faces. And Mr. Vanderpool was on his feet again, calling for people to sign the petition, and they were dutifully falling into line. Perhaps a dozen people got up and left the hall immediately.

Clint was filled with a painful sadness as he left the hall and went to the car. His hope had shattered against the indifference of the crowd. But Dr. McCray was in good spirits. "I think I reached a few of them," he said. "Some left without signing the petition."

Clint wagged his head. "If people are that hard to convince, we've sure got a long way to go."

"Yes," Dr. McCray agreed quietly. "We've got a long way to go. That's why we've got to keep plugging away."

CHAPTER ELEVEN

CLINT AND JUDY sat in the warm kitchen at Judy's home and drank coffee. They had been downtown, but the Malt Shop had been so crowded that they had decided to come home. Anyway, Clint was a little weary of trying to smile at all the remarks that were made about his black eye.

During the Monroe–Eaton game that afternoon, somebody had jammed an elbow in Clint's eye during a pile-up. Now the skin below his right eye was purple. Judy had said that it made him look like a pirate. "All you need is a bandanna on your head."

It had been a close, hard-fought game. The toughest game of the season except for the Stratford battle. Eaton's defensive line had been very hard to crack. If it hadn't been for Clint's hard running and Paul's pile-driving plunges into the line, they'd have made little yardage on the ground. The fact that they had won over Eaton by a score of 19–13 had been primarily due to the passing combination of Tracy to Washington. It had accounted for two of the three touchdowns that the Cougars had made against the Eaton team.

It looked as though Monroe was going to be a passing team in the coming big game between Monroe and Norwalk. The Mustangs had a powerful defensive line too. They were still undefeated and headed the conference rating. Monroe was in second place with one loss. If the Cougars beat the Mustangs in the coming game, they would be co-champions of the conference.

The house was quiet as Clint and Judy sat and sipped their coffee. Mr. and Mrs. Harlin and Debby had gone to a movie. Clint was tired but pleasantly relaxed in his chair. He was thinking what a good thing his nearness to Judy had been during the last two months. During that time he had faced more real problems than he had encountered before in his whole life. And Judy's friendship had helped a lot.

Her voice brought him out of his reverie. "Well, they're going to try it again," she said. "This time I hope to heaven that nothing goes wrong."

"You mean the Washingtons?"

She nodded. "Did Jeff tell you?"

"Yeah. He said that they were going to start moving in in the morning. They've hired a trailer and they're ready to start early. I'm going out and pick up Paul and we're going to help."

A frown creased her forehead. "Do you think anything will happen? Do you think a crowd will gather and try to start trouble?"

He grinned wryly. "It will be a Sunday morning. They should have better manners than to start trouble on a Sunday morning. I don't know," he said. "I've kind of got the feeling that there won't be any trouble. You know, that meeting they had last week was a flop. They got quite a few signatures on the petition, all right, but the petition hasn't made much of an impression. And it hasn't scared out the Washingtons."

They sat in silence for a few moments, and the distant mournful wail of a siren reached them. It gradually grew louder.

"It sounds as if it's coming in this direction," Judy said.

Clint made an old joke. "Probably some cops coming home to dinner."

But as the sound neared, they sat straight in their chairs and concentrated their attention on it. And Clint knew that it was no police siren. It was too deep-pitched and loud for that. Now they could hear the roar of powerful engines. It was the sound of fire engines. It seemed to be coming right to their house. But then, as the sirens began to die, they could place the general direction of the engine sounds.

Clint's pulse quickened and Judy jumped to her feet as the same thought struck them. "Oh, no!" Judy cried, and she ran to the bedroom for a coat. Clint got to his feet and grabbed his sweater.

They hurried out of the house and down the sidewalk. They could already see the flames above the rooftops. They broke into a run. And as they rounded the corner, their fears were realized. It was the Washington house.

Chasing fire engines was a popular pastime for a lot of people in Monroe, and already a curious crowd was beginning to gather, hurrying up the street from parked cars and houses. Two police cars had arrived on the scene, red lights revolving on their tops, and the policemen were busy keeping people back and out of the firemen's way. There were hoarse shouts, smoke, confusion, excitement.

Clint and Judy went directly across the street from the house and watched things from there. Flames were shooting out through the roof of the house, but from where he stood, Clint could see no fire in the lower rooms.

"The fire is in the attic," he told Judy. "Maybe they can get it out before the whole thing burns down."

She had hold of his arm and he looked down at her. Her lips were tight as she fought back the tears.

Firemen on ladders were chopping holes in the roof while others played powerful streams of water on the flames that were visible. Then hoses were passed to the men on the ladders and water roared through the holes in the roof. Smoke boiled out in clouds then, and the flames would disappear for a moment, only to burst out again in small explosions. There was coughing in the crowd.

It took a long time, but the flames gradually died.

Now the area was lighted by headlights on the police cars and searchlights on the fire engines. Clint had been so intent on the fire that he had paid no attention to the crowd that had gathered on the sidewalk where he and Judy stood. He looked at them now, their faces still awed and excited in the pale glow. Then he heard a familiar voice—a loud, aggrieved, protesting voice.

"I suppose we'll be accused of starting it, but we didn't. It wouldn't make much sense for us to start a fire and take a chance on burning down our own houses, would it? I turned in the alarm. That ought to prove that I didn't have anything to do with it. I was in bed and I looked out the window and saw that the place was burning—"

Clint located the owner of the voice. It was Mr. Pfost in slippers and bathrobe, worriedly sucking on the stem of his cold pipe.

Of a sudden, all the pent-up anger that Clint had felt for weeks came out in a rush of words. "Oh, sure!" he said with bitter scorn. "You're innocent, Pfost. You and your crowd did everything you could to get people stirred up in this matter, and then when something happens you start hollering about your innocence. You know what? If that fire had gotten out of control and burned the Washington house to the ground, I'd have hoped your house had burned too."

He was standing before the crowd, his fists clenched, and he knew that if anyone jeered at him or made a smart remark he'd start swinging. He was that mad. But to his surprise, some of them cheered him and there was even laughter, but it was at Mr. Pfost. Then Clint felt a hand on his shoulder that turned him gently but firmly around. He looked into Dr. McCray's face. "Take it easy, Clint."

Clint shrugged. "Sure. I've had my say." He stepped back up on the sidewalk and the people pushed back respectfully to make a place for him.

"Are any of the Washingtons here?" Dr. McCray asked.

"I haven't seen any of them," Clint replied.

"I think I'll go and tell them. Maybe I can break it to them sort of easy."

"It will break their hearts, no matter what you say," Judy put in.

"Would you like to come with me, Judy?"

"All right," she said.

Before they left, the minister put his hand on Clint's shoulder. "Do me a favor?"

"Sure."

"Everybody is taking it for granted that the fire was set. But it could have just happened. There might be angry words before this crowd breaks up. That won't do any good. You've got a steady brain. Try to cool them down."

Clint responded to the compliment. He grinned. "All right. I'll try."

The fire was under control. The smoke was disappearing and the firemen were rolling up the canvas hoses. A policeman was saying, "It's all over, folks. Might as well go home."

Clint made no move to go. He found Archie Strong beside him. "Maybe it isn't so bad, after all," Archie said. "Only the roof is burned."

"There'll be a lot of water damage," Clint declared. "All that water going into the attic. The ceiling and walls will be ruined."

The crowd was thinning out. Everywhere, Clint heard voices saying, "I'll bet someone set it. . . . It's just too much of a coincidence that it happened to-night. . . . Who do you suppose did it? . . ."

But no arguments broke out. Clint guessed that the anti-Washington people were keeping mum. It looked as though it was all over. All over except for the Washingtons, that is.

He heard Mr. Pfost speaking again. There was a sad note in Mr. Pfost's voice. "Maybe some misguided fool did this, but I don't think it was anyone we know. I hope they catch the guy that did it, if someone did start the fire. I feel terrible about this—"

Clint turned and walked over to where Mr. Pfost was talking with his friends. "Do you mean that, Mr. Pfost?"

Mr. Pfost stared at Clint for a moment. His face looked old and tired. "I mean it. I wish I had never gotten mixed up in the situation. If the Washingtons still want to move in, it's all right with me."

"How would you like to help a little?"

"All right. What do you suggest?"

"Soon as the firemen leave we should get in there and clean up. We've got to get the water off those floors. We'll need brooms and mops and rags."

Mr. Pfost nodded. "I'll get the things. And I'll ask the neighbors to help." He walked resolutely toward the house, the folds of his bathrobe flapping about his legs.

Clint's father showed up, and Clint located more of the football gang. As soon as the firemen moved out, they moved in. Gasoline lanterns, part of someone's camping equipment, were lighted and set up in the house. Mr. Pfost had gathered plenty of brooms and mops. Clint removed his shoes and rolled his trousers legs above the knee and grabbed a broom and went to work.

There were gallons of water on the floors. More water dripped from the ceiling and wallpaper hung down in long sodden strips. The stink of wet charred wood was in the air.

Dr. McCray and Judy returned, and Jeff was with them. Jeff was dreary-mouthed, his eyes heavy with pain. When Clint spoke to him, he did not answer. He said nothing at all. He just wandered from room to room with a flashlight and stared at ceilings and walls and floors.

Finally the floors were as dry as mops and rags could make them. It was late and Clint was very tired. His eyes burned and his feet were sore. There was nothing more they could do tonight, so Clint took his shoes outside and crossed the street where the walks were dry. He sat down and put on his shoes. Now that it was all over, the darkness and the cold made him feel discouraged. He began to shiver. He heard a sound and looked up to see Judy standing there.

"You get home and go to bed," she said. "I don't want a pneumonia case on my hands."

He grinned. "All right, ma'am. Anything you say."

Jeff did not show up for football practice on Monday afternoon. Clint and Paul talked about him in the dressing room.

"I guess it was quite a blow to him," Clint was saying. "It will take a lot of work to get the house fixed up again. I didn't think he'd quit football now. Anyway, they have insurance that will cover the damage, haven't they?"

Paul nodded. "All they'll really be out is the time it takes to repair the place. Someone told me that the people in the neighborhood feel bad about what happened, and they're actually anxious to have the Washingtons move in."

"Yeah. I heard that too. It's funny how they changed their minds so fast."

"That's the way people are. You could argue with them until you were black in the face and not get anywhere. But something that shocks them, like that fire, gets results. Maybe they feel guilty. I told Jeff that the whole thing might have been a blessing in disguise. But he can't see it that way. He's been walking a tightrope all along, and the smallest push would have tripped him up. This was a big push. He's fed up with the whole business. I suppose that quitting football is his way of getting even."

"Maybe he's just kind of dazed. Maybe he'll get over it."

"I don't know, Clint. We'll just have to wait and see. But it wouldn't do any good to argue with him now. It's his fight, and for his own good he'll have to handle it alone. He may make it—he may not."

"If he doesn't come back we don't stand a chance of winning the Norwalk game," Clint gritted. He jerked so hard on a shoestring that it broke, and he flung the broken end angrily away. "They're too powerful for us on the ground. We can only beat them through the air."

"I'm afraid you're right, Clint."

"Doggone the contrariness of things, anyway! They didn't want the Washingtons to move in when they wanted to move in. Now, they're willing, and the Washingtons balk."

The days sped by, and Jeff did not come to practice. In the halls and classrooms he was the old-time Jeff. His face was deadpan, and he was so withdrawn inside himself that he hardly seemed to be part of the scene. And they left him alone.

Clint had heard that Mr. Pfost and some of the neighbors were working nights on the Washington house, gradually repairing the damage.

Friday afternoon came, and the light, pre-game work-out, and it was a grim squad that faced the big game tomorrow. They felt like orphans, they'd had so much trouble. From all accounts, the Norwalk team had no troubles, not even injuries. They were rolling along on a tide of prosperity, taking it for granted that they would win, cocksure to the point of arrogance.

After practice, Clint got a real surprise when he looked at the group on the sideline and saw Ralph standing there. Ralph had on a red wool jacket and he stood with hands jammed into pockets, his face solemn. On an impulse, Clint walked over to see him.

Ralph grinned at him, and there was even a trace of shyness in it. "You guys look pretty good out there," he said.

"Sure," Clint agreed. "What there is of us. But I'm afraid we've lost one player too many. Right now, we're no match for Norwalk."

"That's no way to talk, Clint."

"I'm just facing facts."

Ralph took his hands from his pockets and began to pound a fist into a palm nervously.

Clint said, "Well, I've got to get that shower—"

"Wait a minute," Ralph said. While Clint waited, he gazed around a few moments and said slowly, "I've been wanting to talk to you. Maybe I've been wrong about Jeff. Anyway, I hope you don't think I or my dad had anything to do with that fire. Sure, I planted those guys in the stands to boo Jeff at the Kimball game. But house-burning is out of my line."

Clint looked away. "I never thought you did it."

"Dad is furnishing the lumber for the repair work. The Washingtons won't be bothered if they move in now."

"Has your dad changed his mind about the Washingtons, too?"

Ralph shrugged his shoulders expressively. "Dad's too old to change his ideas. He'll be growling about this problem for the next ten years. But he's resigned to it."

Clint looked into Ralph's eyes. "Why don't you tell the coach how you feel? He's a reasonable guy. He'll take you back, and Jim Davis and the others too, if they've changed their ideas. And we'll win that game tomorrow. I'd sure like to win that game."

Ralph's eyes were bleak. "Too late. I've been lying around for three weeks and I'm soft again. So are the other guys. We wouldn't be much help. Anyway, Jim won't come back. You know why he was with me? Because he hated Slansky. Because Slansky pushed him into the second-string, and Jim can't stand being second."

"Well, it's sure funny how things have worked out."

"Yeah." Ralph stuck out his hand and his eyes offered friendship. Clint did not hesitate. He took Ralph's hand in his own.

"Friends again?" Ralph said. "Maybe we'll go to college together yet, and get a new start."

"Sure," Clint agreed.

CHAPTER TWELVE

THE NOVEMBER SUN shone on the bus parked outside the gym. The sky was cloudless and blue, the air crisp and bracing. In the sun's feeble warmth, the Cougar football squad stood around, talking quietly. Then Sullivan and Tucker, in topcoats and hats, came from the building. The boys began to climb the steps into the bus, each one carrying his football gear.

Clint found a seat near the front and sat down heavily. He felt empty and he did not know why. This was it—the big game. This was what they had continually made sacrifices for. He should have been keyed up, but he wasn't. He had no pleasant sense of anticipation, as he usually had before a game. He guessed it was because, deep inside, he felt they were going to lose. All the newspapers and sportscasters said so, and he was inclined to the belief that they might be right. He had tried to argue himself out of the notion, but had fallen victim to his own doubt and the opinions of others.

In fact, defeatism had insidiously seeped through the

whole squad. Coach Sullivan had fought against it, but could not control it. Clint could feel the mood now. Sure, some of the fellows were talking loud and boisterously, but that didn't mean anything. The general atmosphere was all wrong.

Clint blamed it all on Jeff. Jeff was the one player who was good enough to tip the scales in Monroe's favor in the coming battle. But Jeff wasn't here.

The trouble went even deeper than that. There were a good number of players who had become personally concerned with Jeff's problem. They had even come to identify themselves with his struggle. There were those who had helped put the windows in the Washington house, those who had gone to the meeting with Dr. McCray, and those who had helped clean up after the fire. They had become more deeply involved than they realized. And they had grown to like the tall Negro boy with his soft drawl, and the slow smile that waved over his face when something pleased him. They missed him.

Now, it looked as though misfortune had gotten Jeff down, and his defeat was their defeat. Sure, he had had a tough row to hoe—you couldn't deny that—but neither could you deny that he had let his troubles beat him. It had an effect on the whole team, for right up until the present moment, many of them had cherished a secret hope that he would come back.

Only Paul still believed in Jeff. He had brought along Jeff's football gear—just in case.

Suited up in the dressing room at Cougar Bowl, they stood and listened to last-minute instructions from Coach Sullivan. He didn't say much about the Norwalk team. Norwalk's strengths and weaknesses had been drilled into them all week long on the practice field.

Sullivan was trying to break through their apathy and strike some fire. He intimated, without actually saying it, that they were short on guts. He told them that they were letting him down. He said that they were betraying the team, the school, and themselves. But he failed to strike the right chord, and nothing he said had the desired effect.

Finally, he relaxed his strained attitude. "All I'm asking is that you do your best, and the rest doesn't matter. Everybody out!"

On the field for the warm-up, Clint scuffed his feet on the brown turf. It was hard and dry, but not yet frozen. He was thankful. Frozen turf could feel like concrete when you hit it. Between passes, his eyes roved about. There was a sell-out crowd in the stands, and the tiered bleachers dazzled with light and color. The crowd's noise was a continuous thing, rising and falling in waves. He thought of Judy up there and decided that he was playing for her as well as for the team. He began to feel alive.

He gazed downfield at the Mustangs, looking big and top-heavy in their pads and green jerseys, and he felt a strong antagonism. The publicity in favor of the powerful Mustangs during the past week had cowed him, but it had also galled him. The role of the under-dog had been forced on Monroe. No, he didn't like it at all. He knew now that he'd play hard and give his best no matter what the odds were against them. But he wasn't so sure about some of the other fellows.

There weren't more than a couple of minutes left in the warm-up period when he heard a smattering of applause in the Monroe stands. Then the applause grew into a roar, and the squad paused and looked in surprise.

"Well, I'll be darned," Walt said. "Look there!"

Legging it down the sideline toward Sullivan, carry-ing his helmet under his arm, his dark face identifying him to everyone, was Jeff. Practically everyone in the Monroe stands knew Jeff's story, and his sudden appear-ance had stirred a sentiment in their hearts. They gave him a standing ovation. Clint felt like cheering, too.

Jeff talked with Sullivan for a moment and then came running onto the field. More than glad to see him, the players pretended indifference. There was just a tinge of anger in their attitude. He had kept them in suspense too long.

"Well, what happened to you?" Clint said, as Jeff came loping up.

Jeff made an unexpected confession. "I decided that I was acting like a kid. I'm over that. Sorry, fellas, I'll try to make it up to you."

Walt clapped his hands together. "All right, gang, let's go!"

A new feeling, a quality of spirit, came into the squad and they played with speed and fire. Clint looked down-field at the green jerseys and said, "Hah!"

When they moved off the field, Jeff said to Clint, "How about it, Clint boy, are you going to help us move in tomorrow morning?"

"Sure thing, Jeff," Clint said, his feeling strong in his words.

Jeff flashed his white teeth. "It's not all fixed up yet, but we can live in it. We'll get her fixed."

"Sure you will." And Clint realized that, in spite of Jeff's upsets, the boy had a plodding determination that would work things out all right.

The Mustangs won the toss of the coin and chose to receive. Soon the high musical note of the referee's whistle sounded, and Paul skipped a step and broke into a run for the kickoff. The ball soared deep into Mustang territory where a back snatched it out of the air and started away, gold satin-clad legs moving in a blur of speed. Jeff tripped him up on the Mustang 35.

But then it looked as though the Cougars had waited too long to get organized. They were forced to retreat before the Mustang offense. The green backs plunged through openings in the line, or skirted the ends with terrible speed. Ten yards . . . seven yards . . . twelve yards . . . they tore it off in chunks. The Cougars had a few terrible minutes of something like panic. Maybe it was true. Maybe they were unstoppable.

It was Jeff who woke them up and got them functioning as a defensive unit. It was Jeff who had cutting words to say when someone missed a tackle, and coming from him it seemed funny. Maybe they wouldn't have taken it if he hadn't been so good himself. Here he hadn't been in uniform for over a week, and he was making the rest of them look like beginners. A subtle instinct seemed to tell him which way a play was going, and he was sneaking through the interference and stopping ball-carriers before they really broke loose.

"How about giving me a little help?" he taunted them, as Archie called the defensive signal and they moved into formation.

The Mustangs charged with increased vigor as they neared the goal line, but the Cougar defense had stiffened. They stopped the green jerseys cold on their own ten-yard line, and took over on downs. Paul coolly kicked out of danger. Jeff was down fast with the flight of the ball, and the Mustang safety signaled a fair catch on the 35. Then they held Norwalk to a gain of five yards in three tries, and the Mustangs kicked on fourth down. It was a wobbly boot, just over the heads of the secondary, and Walt scooped it up on the 25 and ran like mad. He was hit hard on the 40.

They started upstream, fighting against the green tide. It was mighty rough going, but they tore off steady yardage.

"Let's go—team! . . . Let's go—team! . . . Let's go!" the Monroe rooters chanted gleefully.

Clint took the ball on a hand-off and headed wide

around left end. The defensive right end almost got him, but Bill Montgomery threw a block just in time. Clint ran as fast as he could, flying breathlessly across the chalk stripes, until somebody hit him from behind. He plowed a furrow in the turf with his helmet and rolled over and got to his feet. He had picked up seventeen yards. He was glowing inside and he felt mighty tall as he went back to the huddle.

"That's the way to go, gang!"

The signals, the clash of padded bodies, the blaze of speed as Bill Montgomery smacked the left side of the line. Five yards gained . . . two yards . . . three. First down. The will to win drove them to unsparing effort. They would not be stopped.

They plowed their way to the Mustang 20 before Walt called a pass play. It would be a pass into the end zone, Jeff receiving.

The ball was snapped. Walt danced around behind his protection, waiting for the moment, the precise moment, to throw the ball. His arm shot forward. There was a man in front of Jeff, but Jeff had the reach on him by inches. He made it look absurdly easy as he took the ball in his big hands. As the Monroe stands burst into a roar, he tossed the ball lightly to the referee and went back to the huddle as casually as if he were out for a Sunday stroll.

When Paul put the ball between the uprights for the extra point and the big 7 went up on the scoreboard, Clint felt a grim satisfaction. The knowledge that they could score against the Mustangs had destroyed the myth of their invincibility. They could beat these guys! It was going to be tough, but it could be done. He looked at the green jerseys heading downfield, and he thought, "You've had your own way too long, boys."

The Cougars held their seven-point lead until just before the end of the half. Then the touchdown that the Norwalk rooters seemed sure was coming, finally came. A Mustang halfback broke loose, and by some magic of maneuver and speed, ran through the whole Cougar team for a TD. In spite of frantic efforts to stop him, he covered fifty yards, a thrilling run that brought the fans to their feet yelling. The Mustangs converted, too, and the score was tied at 7–7.

The score was unchanged at the end of the third quarter. As the teams changed ends of the field for the start of the fourth quarter, Clint looked at his teammates. Dirty, sweating, faces scratched, jerseys torn, they looked like the battling team that they were. There had been numerous replacements, but some of them were beginning to tire. If they could keep up the fight . . .

They hurled their offense at the unbeaten Mustangs. There weren't many flaws in the Norwalk defense, but what there were Walt's keen mind exploited. The Cougars played like men possessed. They gained ground, only to lose it all when Bill Montgomery fumbled on the Mustang 15, and a green jersey recovered. Bill was so mad he was ready to bawl. He had been playing his heart out. The Mustangs kicked, and the Cougars started the long weary trek all over again.

On their own 35, Walt called for a pass play that they did not often use—a long, all-or-nothing pass whose success depended on Walt's throwing arm and Jeff's speed.

"Let's go!"

The ball was snapped. The defense charged. Walt spun and faked a pitch-out to Bill. Over on the right, Jeff had slipped between the defensive end and tackle and was picking up speed downfield. Fading deep, Walt faked a hand-off to Clint, and Clint bent over and headed for the middle of the line.

Jeff's long graceful stride had taken him past the secondary now. Walt was well protected as he heaved a long one down the middle. The ball lifted and soared. Jeff took it on the Mustang's 30 and streaked for the goal line. Two green jerseys were right behind him, but they couldn't gain a step. Jeff flashed ahead and went over for the TD standing up.

The roar from the stands had not even begun to diminish as they lined up for the conversion attempt. The goal posts stood out against the deep blue of the sky. The snap, the place, the kick. The ball made a low arc—too low! It struck the crossbar squarely in center and bounced back. Paul covered his face with his hands and muttered some bitter words.

"If I had tried to do that, I'd never have made it in a hundred tries!" he wailed.

"It's all right, Paul," Clint said. And maybe it was. They led by 13–7.

After that Clint had never played in such a fierce game. With time running low, the Mustangs took the kickoff and headed for the far goal line with a deliberate, cold fury. Fatigue was beginning to get its leaden grip on the Cougar defenders and the Mustangs were ripping off yardage. Maybe the Mustangs were just as tired, but it did not seem to be so. Between plays the red jerseys shifted on tired feet and stood and blew. The stands were in a continual uproar, but the players were deaf to the noise. Clint called on his flagging resources to help stop the drive. They had to protect their narrow lead. A TD and an extra point would beat them. Clint could not bear the thought of losing.

Time was very low when the green team reached the Cougar 40. "Watch for a pass!" Walt called excitedly.

The Mustang quarterback faded to pass, but could find no receivers. He saw a chance to run for it, and he did! He tucked the ball under his arm and ran wide to the left. Blockers cleared a path for him. He left would-be tacklers strewn behind him, and picked up speed. It looked as though he was going to shake loose!

Clint was moving over to his right. He had to stop that man! A blocker lunged at him. He used his hands and side-stepped and got out of the way of the hurtling body. Except for Clint, the rocketing quarterback was in the clear. He was going down the sideline a mile a minute. Clint angled toward him, calling on everything he had for one final effort. And in those brief moments, he felt the old coolness inside him, the confidence he had won, which he could not explain but only feel. He threw all the strength of his body at the ball-carrier's midsection and the runner toppled as though he had hit a post. They rolled out of bounds together. Clint bounced to his feet and wiped a trickle of blood away from a scratch over his eye.

The referee moved the ball in-bounds one third the width of the field. The Mustang back had made it to the 25. Time for one—maybe two plays. The green team moved quickly from the huddle to the line of scrimmage. Desperate, the Mustangs took to the air. The quarterback threw a pass which sailed past the hands of the intended receiver. Another pass. The gun cracked when the ball was in the air. Jeff leaped high and slapped the leather to the ground. The game was over. The big green team was beaten. The score: 13–7. The Norwalk stands were deathly quiet, numbed by the defeat of a team they had believed unbeatable.

The Monroe crowd moved down the stands like a tide and washed over the field in an overflow. The band, completely disorganized, was playing merrily as individuals. There were happy shouts. The hero-worshipers hoisted players onto their shoulders and paraded them around. Clint was suddenly very tired, but his heart beat with a deep, joyful rhythm. He shouldered his way through the mob in the general direction of the dressing room, helmet in hand, his hair rumpled and wet and plastered to his forehead.

The sun hung orange and crimson above the rim of the stadium, but in the chill shadows the faces were a blur. Then he felt an arm thrown over his shoulder and he turned his head to look at Jeff. There was a happy shine in Jeff's dark eyes.

"Feels pretty good to be a winner, doesn't it, Clint boy?"

"Sure does, Jeff."

Jeff winked at him. "I've been thinking, Clint. With you down at Judy's place so much, we're going to be practically neighbors, eh?"

Clint laughed. "That's right. We'll be seeing a lot of each other."

Together they headed for the dressing room and the luxury of hot showers.

About the Author

ALTHOUGH GILBERT DOUGLAS has traveled to many interesting places, the Boise Valley of Idaho is where he has spent most of his life, and where he likes best to live. He grew up on a farm there, and his family before him. His grandfather was an Idaho sheriff and gold miner, and his great-grandfather was one of the early Idaho settlers. Mr. Douglas is proud of his native state and, whenever possible, he likes to visit its spots of historic interest.

Mr. Douglas enjoys all kinds of sports—from swimming to track meets. In high school he played football and basketball. Later, at the University of Washington, he was a freshman manager of the varsity football team.

His other hobbies are reading and fishing. In the summertime he likes to pitch a tent in the Boise Mountains and live out-of-doors, catching trout in the mountain streams and cooking them over an open fire.

He spent five years with the United States Marines, serving in the Philippine Islands and Shanghai. He has also been a logger and a truck driver and has worked in the bunkers of a coal mine. His home is in Nampa, Idaho.